# MINE TO LOVE

## SAFE HARBOR SERIES

## JEN TALTY

JUPITER PRESS

# PRAISE FOR JEN TALTY

*"Deadly Secrets* is the best of romance and suspense in one hot read!" *NYT Bestselling Author Jennifer Probst*

"A charming setting and a steamy couple heat up the pages in a suspenseful story I couldn't put down!" *NY Times and USA today Bestselling Author Donna Grant*

"Jen Talty's books will grab your attention and pull you into a world of relatable characters, strong personalities, humor, and believable sto-rylines. You'll laugh, you'll cry, and you'll rush to get the next book she releases!" Natalie Ann USA Today Bestselling Author

"I positively loved *In Two Weeks*, and highly recommend it. The writing is wonderful, the story is fantastic, and the characters will keep you coming back for more. I can't wait to get my hands on future installments of the NYS Troopers series." *Long and Short Reviews*

"*In Two Weeks* hooks the reader from page one. This is a fast paced story where the development of the romance grabs you emotionally and the suspense keeps you sitting on the edge of your chair. Great characters, great writing, and a believable plot that can be a warning to all of us." *Desiree Holt, USA Today Bestseller*

"*Dark Water* delivers an engaging portrait of wounded hearts as the memorable characters take you on a healing journey of love. A mysterious death brings danger and intrigue into the drama, while sultry passions brew into a believable plot that melts the reader's heart. Jen Talty pens an entertaining romance that grips the heart as the colorful and dangerous story unfolds into a chilling ending." *Night Owl Reviews*

"This is not the typical love story, nor is it the typical mystery. The characters are well rounded and interesting." *You Gotta Read Reviews*

"*Murder in Paradise Bay* is a fast-paced romantic thriller with plenty of twists and turns to keep you guessing until the end. You won't want to miss this one..." *USA Today bestselling author Janice Maynard*

# BOOK DESCRIPTION

**Everyone needs a safe harbor to sail into.**

**In this gripping tale of mystery, suspense, and the power of love, Miles and Liberty will face unimaginable challenges and make sacrifices to bring justice to Lighthouse Cove.**

Miles Kirby leads a double life. By day, he's a skilled mechanic, fixing engines and tinkering with gadgets. But by night, he becomes a relentless private investigator, delving into the shadows to uncover the truth.

Living next door to Miles is Liberty Blue, a young woman burdened with caring for her younger brother, who is on the autism spectrum. Their lives intersect unexpectedly when Liberty's brother mysteriously vanishes without a trace.

Driven by compassion and a sense of duty, Miles takes it upon himself to find Liberty's missing brother. As he dives deeper into the investigation, he uncovers a web of secrets and dangerous connections that threaten to unravel the very fabric of Lighthouse Cove.

As the stakes rise and danger lurks at every turn, Miles and Liberty must confront their fears and face the truth that sometimes, the ones we trust the most may be hiding the darkest secrets. In a race against the clock, they must rely on their wits, resilience, and the unexpected bond that forms between them.

*For everyone who feels a little different.*

*M*iles Kirby snagged a glass of bourbon and strolled to the other side of the pool. The sun beat down on his face. Thank God his brother and his bride hadn't required ties at this wedding. If they had, Miles would have not only been sweating, but he would have been uncomfortable as hell. It was bad enough his mother demanded he wear a decent pair of slacks and a button-down shirt versus his usual jeans and T-shirt, which considering this had been a family only event, it would have been fine. But to avoid the argument, he did what his mother requested.

He glanced over his shoulder and smiled. Emmerson was a lucky man and Miles was damn happy for his brother. But all these weddings and babies had certainly put Miles in a funk.

Or perhaps it had been something else.

He'd spent the entire day trying not to think about his sexy neighbor, but try as he might, she was all he could think about. It drove him batshit crazy. The woman had turned him down every single time he asked her out and part of him understood why.

Didn't make the rejection any easier to swallow.

His entire family had surrounded the happy couple. There was laughter and tears of joy.

"Here's to Emmerson and Rumor," his father said with a raised flute.

His brother and his new bride were so disgusting sometimes it made Miles want to gag. Only, his heart had a different reaction. It swelled with pride and bliss for his brother, it truly did.

But now Miles was the last man standing. The only Kirby boy who wasn't married. How dare all his brothers run off and tie the knot.

To make matters worse, Emmerson's new bride was expecting their first child. Now he was the only one left who didn't have a kid. Or two. Or three. Well, Emmett was still waiting for that miracle to happen, but this time the adoption would come through. Miles just knew it.

But with all these flipping babies, his mother seemed to more than enjoy reminding him of his single status every chance she got. It had never bothered him before. He could always shrug it off because he didn't care about such things. Sharing a bed for anything other than mutual gratification wasn't in his wheelhouse. He didn't have the bandwidth for relationships. Nor the tolerance. Not because he wasn't a caring man. He was. But he liked his life simple. Without complications. And women complicated the fuck out of it.

And there was that other thing. The thing that reminded him he wasn't good enough.

But he constantly told himself it wasn't that. It was the entanglement of a lady and being tied down. He'd attempted it once. And it had gone to shit before it really got off the ground. It wasn't worth it. For more than one reason.

Sure, all of his sisters-in-law were great women who complemented his brothers, not ruled their lives. He and all his brothers still got together for poker nights. They went fishing. Did all the things they did before marriage and kids.

But it wasn't as often and there were times family life just got in the way. He couldn't begrudge his brothers that. Besides, he loved his nieces and nephews. And all his sisters-in-law. He enjoyed the big family barbecues and birthday parties. Every last one of them.

Only now, he was the last single man and everyone looked at him differently, even though his brothers said they didn't. He knew damn well Seth and Nathan thought he was nuts. They couldn't understand his aversion to being in a relationship and lately, neither could he.

The rest of his brothers? Well, they sort of got it. But only because they'd been sucker punched in the gut by a woman, leaving them brokenhearted.

That had never happened to Miles. Not even by Trixi and he had cared about her. A lot. More than anyone else he'd ever dated. But he knew nothing of love. Had never experienced it. Wasn't sure he ever wanted to, in part, thanks to his mother and those of his brothers who had their souls stomped on.

However, it was more than that and Miles chose to ignore the real reason he never allowed himself to get serious. The one time he came close, he got reminded real fast of all the reasons he'd never make for a good husband. Or father.

He eased into a chair at the table on the far side of the pool and stared at Emmerson and Rumor. He knew the pains they had gone through to get to this moment. Rumor was damn fucking lucky to be alive. Poor girl had been running from bad guys for fifteen years, constantly looking over her shoulder, until she landed in Lighthouse Cove.

Thank God for small favors.

This had truly been her safe harbor, as it had been for all of his sisters-in-law.

The sun hung high over the big beach house, owned by Miles' mom and her second husband. It had been a picture-perfect day for a poolside wedding in front of the ocean. Miles watched as Emmerson kissed his new wife with his hand firmly planted on her midsection. Emmerson would make for a great father, and he couldn't have picked a better woman to share in parenthood. The man deserved a bit of happiness in his life, especially when it came to women. That man, in the past, had piss-poor taste when it came to choosing ladies for long-term relationships.

And he wasn't any better at finding the right ones for friends with benefits either.

That's because Emmerson was the kind of man who needed a partner, only it took him his entire life to mend a broken heart and let a woman like Rumor heal it.

While Rumor hadn't an easy start to her life in Lighthouse Cove, and she came with her own wounds and set of baggage, she was exactly what Emmerson needed and they made for a spectacular couple. Even Miles could see that.

He was truly thrilled for them and wanted the best for their growing family.

But it didn't change the sudden shift in his emotions. He'd been a confirmed bachelor his entire life. Unlike all of his brothers, he had thought he never wanted—or deserved—a family. The mere idea had made him break out in hives.

Even when he turned forty, he still didn't want to settle down.

Yet the second Rumor stole his brother's heart, everything shifted. Miles couldn't figure out why, not that he'd spent too much time trying and he'd certainly not chatted about it with anyone. But he found himself wanting more than a roll in the hay here and a short-lived fling there. Besides, as his family constantly joked, he'd run out of women to date in Lighthouse Cove.

Miles sipped his bourbon and eyed the groom as Emmerson strolled across the pool deck. "Hey, man." Miles lifted his drink. "I don't think I've ever seen you smile so wide before."

"I take it you've heard the good news like everyone else in this family. Before me." Emmerson set his drink on the table and pulled up a chair. "I should be pissed at the lot of you, but that would mean I'd have to be mad at my wife and how could I be angry at that sweet thing."

Miles laughed. "I've seen the two of you fight and you always lose." He slapped his brother on the back. "Congratulations. On both the nuptials and the baby. I couldn't be happier for you."

"Then why are you sitting over here, all by yourself, with a sourpuss look on your face?" Emmerson clanked his drink against Miles' before taking a swig.

Miles had a special relationship with each of his brothers. They all did. And not a single one of them ever got jealous. They were good that way, regardless of age differences. Seth and Nathan, the two oldest, were tight. Miles and Jameson, being the two youngest, had their own bond. The three in the middle, Rhett, Emmett, and Emmerson, had been as thick as thieves growing up.

But that didn't stop each of them developing side relationships. And Miles and Emmerson had been each other's sounding boards for the last couple of years. They owned a boat together. They went on fishing trips together.

However, that had been because they were the two single dudes left.

Not anymore.

"Avoiding Mother." Miles cocked his head. "Now that you've tied the knot, she's in rare form and it's starting to really piss me off."

"I bet she is, which is why Rumor's over there chatting with her about the baby's room." Emmerson leaned in. "Which we have no intention of letting Mom decorate, but Rumor thought you might be avoiding Mom and maybe even Dad too. They shouldn't be putting the pressure on you at our wedding."

"Dad's nowhere near as bad. Actually, he didn't say one word when I didn't bring a date. I think he was pleased that I left the flavor of the month at the ice cream shop. As if I ever brought anyone to a family gathering before. But Mom was all over that shit. She told me the family's lopsided, whatever the fuck that means." Miles didn't mean to sound short. Or even resentful. At least not about himself. This was Emmerson and Rumor's special day. The focus shouldn't be on Miles and his decision to remain single for the rest of his life.

"That's an odd thing to say, even for Mom." Emmerson leaned back in his chair. "I'll say something to her. It's really none of her business and it's obviously got you in a foul mood."

"I'm sorry, man. I don't mean to be. I really don't." He ran a hand over his jaw, letting his thumb and forefinger come to a point at his jaw. He sighed. "You and Rumor might have only been engaged for two weeks, but we all knew a couple of months ago it was only a matter of time. The two of you were talking about it."

"Rumor and I made the decision two months ago. We even had a date in mind. I just wanted to give her a proper proposal. Make it special for her," Emmerson said. "I've been watching what Mom and even Dad have been doing to you and I'm sorry. It's worse than anything she's ever done or said to me." Emmerson held up his hand. "But it's just because you're the only one of us who has ever specifically stated you're never getting married or having kids and while I get your reasons, I don't agree. The rest of us have always wanted it, even if I thought I gave up on the idea."

Miles laughed. "You never gave up on it; you just had to wait for the right woman to knock down your walls."

"That may be true," Emmerson said. "But I have

to ask, and don't get pissed. You haven't dated in months, which isn't like you. What's going on?"

That was a loaded question and one he wasn't sure he really wanted to get into. But it did open the door to a different conversation. "You know, Nathan, Seth, Rhett, and even Emmett have different memories of Mom and Dad's marriage than you, me, and Jameson do."

"What does that have to do with anything?" Emmerson cocked his head.

"They remember the good times. We remember the bullshit."

"That's crap. They were older and saw all of it." Emmerson arched a brow. "And I know where you're going. Nathan and Seth got married young. But so did Jameson."

"Jameson was looking for someone to love him because he didn't feel like he fit in. He just didn't know why. And it was all our mother's fault."

"No. It was Dad's too for lying." Emmerson took a sip of his drink. "None of this has to do with why you're not dipping into any dating pool. It does have a shit ton to do with why you don't do relationships and I'm not even going to start in on that," Emmerson said. "But I thought you were going to ask your neighbor to come today. I told you that Rumor and I were fine with that. Rumor loves working with her at Safe Harbor Café and every time I go in there, she's so sweet. She seems like a really good person. And her brother has a wicked sense of humor for someone on the spectrum."

Leave it to Emmerson to bring up Liberty. The one woman who had turned down the Miles charm. It happened, but it didn't happen often. Miles understood why and her reasons were twofold. Both were reasonable, and both should make him stop trying.

"She's cool." Miles nodded, wondering how much he should tell Emmerson. Not much was kept in the vault when it came to his family. Not because they all gossiped about each other, but because they all cared. He valued that about his family. Loved that about each and every one.

But sometimes it was annoying as fuck.

"She had plans with Gabriel," Miles said. When Miles had strolled across the yards to ask Liberty, she'd mentioned taking Gabriel to the movies, but she hadn't actually said when.

Liberty had moved in two months ago with her special needs little brother, who wasn't so little. Nope. He was a grown-ass man at twenty-two. Funny as hell guy with a sense of humor that had Miles in stitches half the time. It had taken Gabriel a good three weeks to warm up to Miles, but now that he was working at the auto shop, they were like two peas in a pod.

His sister, on the other hand?

She still struggled to understand why Miles enjoyed her brother.

Miles knew what it was like to be an outcast. He'd

struggled all through school because of his learning disabilities, and he'd tried to explain that to Liberty, but they'd been interrupted, yet again, by her fucking prick of an ex-husband.

"I'm sorry she couldn't come, but glad you at least asked." Emmerson lowered his gaze and leaned closer. "You like her and don't try to tell this old man otherwise."

"Old man? Is that what Rumor is calling you these days instead of Mr. Saucy, all because you won't let her—"

"Shut the fuck up." Emmerson shook his head before dropping it back and downing the last drop of his drink. "This family's obsession with my sex life is fucking weird."

"Only because you're the one who constantly got caught with his pants down when we were kids."

Emmerson held up three fingers. "Three damn times and no one will ever let me live it down, including my wife."

"She's the best damn thing that has ever happened to you."

"Tell me something I don't know," Emmerson said. "And stop changing the subject. You're so damn good at doing that, it drives me crazy. We're talking about you. And Liberty."

Miles lifted his drink and took a long slow slip. He swirled it around in his mouth, letting his taste buds get their fill of the rich wood flavor before swallowing. "There's nothing to discuss."

"I don't believe that for one minute. As a matter of fact, I think she's more the reason you're sitting over here by yourself than Mom's insanity."

Emmerson was only half-right because their mother had gotten under Miles' skin with her constant badgering. The only question was, would Miles own it?

Fuck it. He could at least tell his brother some of it, although Emmerson didn't need a recantation of Miles' insecurities. Emmerson already knew and had chimed in his two cents years ago.

"Her ex-husband keeps coming around," Miles said. "She doesn't seem to like that or him. But she puts up with it because of Gabriel."

"Ah, I see. He's put a damper on anything happening between you and Liberty." Emmerson nodded. "That would put me in a shitty mood too."

"It's more than that. It's her little brother. He adores Charlie and because of how Gabriel is, Liberty can't break that bond. I respect that, but I can see the pain in that girl's eyes and it's got my mind and my gut going down a dangerous path. I can't put a lid on it, even though it's none of my damn business."

"Do you know why they got divorced?"

Miles shook his head. "I've never had the chance to talk with her that long or have a deep conversation. But it doesn't matter. I'm going to have to let this one go. Besides, even if something did happen between us, it's not like it would go anywhere. We all know what I'm like and long-haul relationships and me do not mix."

"Don't get pissed, because I'm not being Mom here, but that's bullshit. You choose to be this way, and I'm not judging. Take it from a man who had one foot out the door in every relationship until Rumor and that's exactly what you're doing right now." Emmerson cocked his head. "If you go into anything believing it won't last, then it won't. Trust me, I know that from experience." He tapped his finger on the table. "I'm not trying to tell you what to do or how to live your life. I wouldn't do that to you. But what I am telling you, is that if you like this girl and want to see if you have it in you, then go for it. Otherwise, you'll never know."

Miles shifted in his seat, tugging at his slacks. God, how he hated anything with pleats. His heart fluttered in a manner he wasn't accustomed to. The words his older brother spoke filled his brain and something unfamiliar snaked through his system. No one had ever quite broken it down that way before. Most of his family pushed him hard. Told him he had to be lonely, which he wasn't. Or that he was avoiding life. Again, that's not what he was doing. He had no regrets. Not a single one. He loved every second of how he'd lived right up until a few months ago. He couldn't even say Liberty had been the catalyst, because he'd been feeling this itch before he met her, but she certainly tossed him over the edge.

Emmerson was right. He liked this girl more than he'd liked most. He might have been what most people called a player, but he treated women with respect. All the ladies he dated received his full attention. He was up front with them, telling them he couldn't fully commit. But he wasn't a cheater. He never dated more than one girl at a time, and when he was with someone, that woman was the only one he had eyes for, until it was time to call it quits.

Sure, he'd broken a few hearts. He'd had more than one woman call him a few choice words. One even tossed a lamp at his head when he broke up with her, but he'd let that relationship go on a little too long. And frankly, he deserved a slap across the face for that one. However, he'd honestly truly cared for Trixi. Even if he hadn't ended up being a jerk in the end, her father was right, Miles wasn't good enough for her and he had to accept that fact.

A concept he struggled with when it came to Liberty, and why he was in a sour mood.

But he wasn't as bad as people made him out to be. He didn't have as many ex-girlfriends as the town made it seem. He was just a guy who didn't want to get married, for more than one reason. One of which was, he didn't want to suffer what his father had gone through. Or what some of his brothers had experienced, but witnessing that firsthand had been almost as bad as being the one who had to survive it.

"By that contemplative look on your face, I'd say I struck a chord," Emmerson said softly in that kind and caring voice he had. As kids, Emmerson always knew when to play the asshole older brother, when to be the friend, and when to straddle the two.

This was one of those moments and Emmerson did it well.

"Yeah, you did," Miles admitted. "I'm just not sure what to do about it. There are always two things that get in my way."

"You know what I think of both of them." Emmerson lifted his drink and sipped it with the same arched brow their father had when he was making a point and he knew he was spot-on.

Miles hated that expression on his dad and it was worse on his older brother.

"There's also the fact she could still be hung up on her ex," Miles added for good measure.

"Only one way to find out," Emmerson said.

Miles nodded. "I suppose you're right."

"Enough of the heavy stuff. How's Gabriel working out at the shop?" Emmerson asked.

Miles smiled. He adored that young man. Gabriel would light up like a lightning storm offshore when something clicked in his brain while he was working on a vehicle. It took him a little longer to get there, but sometimes that was half the fun. "He's great when he's under the hood of a car, but struggles when customers come in. I get it. And he'll probably always be like that. He's gotten pretty comfortable with me and everyone else who works for me, so we've devised a system. Anytime he's in the garage, and someone rolls in, he makes a beeline for one of us, instead of letting the customer approach him, because that doesn't always work out well and he ends up feeling horrible. I don't want that for him, and neither do any of my customers, who have been so kind to him."

"I'm glad people are treating him well. He can't help being on the spectrum."

"The thing is, once he's used to you, he's fine. I think something else happened to him along the way, but I don't know that for sure."

"You're a good man for taking him under your wing. Most people wouldn't." Emmerson smiled. "Speaking of which. I need to bring my personal car in for service. Can I do that tomorrow?"

"Of course," Miles said. "But aren't you and Rumor going to take any kind of a honeymoon?"

"I got us a room tonight at Melinda's B and B. In a couple of weeks, we're going down to Key West for a long weekend, if she's feeling up to it. Idiot me thought her getting sick this morning was her having cold feet, not morning sickness. She's still not feeling too great and it's been going on all week. So, we'll have to see how that plays out."

"I sure hope you can go, but having a baby kind of trumps a honeymoon."

"No truer words have been spoken." Emmerson smiled. "I also need to sell my motorcycle."

"No." Miles glared. "Rumor's making you get rid of it?"

"I wouldn't say making me, but she did make some strong arguments about us being parents and I thought it might be time. Besides, I drive it so rarely these days anyway. So, if you want it, I'll give it to you. Otherwise, I thought maybe you could find someone to purchase it."

"My bike riding days ended a few years ago when I crashed mine." Miles laughed, rubbing his knee. That accident had scared the crap out of him. Talk about seeing your life flash before your eyes. "But I'm happy to put a for sale sign on it at the shop. I'm sure it will sell quickly."

"Thanks, man. I appreciate it."

"Anytime." Miles pointed. "Here comes your beautiful bride."

"Hey, babe." Emmerson patted his legs.

Rumor smiled as she wrapped her arm around Emmerson's shoulders and eased onto his lap. "Well, your mother thinks we should name our baby, Emmerson Stephen Dalton Kirby if it's a boy and if it's a girl—"

"Rebecca Alison Maxwell Kirby," Emmerson and

Miles both said at the same time and burst out laughing.

"I don't think it's funny. I'm not naming my child either of those things. First, I don't think your father would appreciate his name taking a back seat to Steve. Second, that's too fucking long and no offense, honey, but we're not having a junior. And third. Really? Rebecca? I love your mom, but has she always been this self-centered and I just missed it? Oh, where does Alison and Maxwell come from? She didn't say."

"Alison is her middle name and Maxwell is her maiden name." Miles waggled his brows. "Welcome to the family, sister-in-law."

"No. Just no." Rumor shook her head.

"I agree." Emmerson kissed his wife's hand. "To all of it. But I do have one request that I'd like to make right here."

"What's that?" Rumor planted a kiss on her husband's cheek.

"That Miles is our child's godfather," Emmerson said proudly.

Miles opened his mouth, but nothing came out. He had eleven nieces and nephews but was not a godfather to any of them. He didn't resent that fact. There were seven brothers. And some of his brothers' wives had other family to consider.

"I love that idea," Rumor said. "What do you say, Miles?"

"I'd be honored." He waggled his finger. "As long as that doesn't require dirty diaper changing."

"Oh. It does. And lots of babysitting." Rumor stood. "Come on, Mr. Saucy. Let's go cut that cake so we can get out of here and head to Melinda's place. I've got some handcuffs with your name on them."

Miles burst out laughing. "If you ever get him in those, this family is going to need pictures as proof."

"Not going to happen." Emmerson took his wife by the hand and meandered toward the other side of the pool.

Miles rose and followed two paces behind. He'd have a piece of cake and say his goodbyes. Time to change his attitude, and his approach.

If he crashed and burned, so be it. At least he'd tried.

Liberty Blue stared at her ex-husband, doing her best to keep her temper in check when she really wanted to tell him to fuck off. When she moved from Palm Beach to Lighthouse Cove, the goal was to put the past behind her and give her and her brother a fresh start. One that didn't include her ex-husband or his family.

She should have known Charlie wouldn't let her go that easily. And now he was using his relationship with her little brother to worm his way into her life.

Fucking asshole.

But she couldn't break Gabriel's heart one more time.

The move had been hard enough. He'd been confused by what felt like the suddenness of it, even though she'd been planning it for months. And then there was her request not to continue contact with Charlie. That had been difficult for Gabriel and in the end, she allowed text messages and a few phone calls, but she asked Gabriel not to give Charlie details and she was to be present.

She thought Gabriel had respected her request, but Charlie must have manipulated Gabriel into doing otherwise.

It wasn't the first time she'd had to deal with people who didn't honestly care about Gabriel.

Their parents' betrayal had nearly destroyed them both.

It had taken years for Gabriel to get over that one, and there were moments when he reverted back to the days when he wanted his mom and dad.

More his father than their mother.

She couldn't blame him for that.

"Come on, Liberty. What's the big deal?" Charlie smiled that cocky grin that used to make her swoon and giggle like a schoolgirl. Not anymore. He no longer had that kind of hold over her and no man ever would. She'd never fall for that kind of charm again. Charlie was the kind of man who made you believe he cared when he didn't. He only cared about himself. No one else.

He never thought she'd leave. No one left Charlie Blue. He was the catch of the county. Handsome. Rich. And every girl wanted him.

But he chose the poor girl tasked with taking care of her little brother with autism.

Something to this day she still didn't understand.

Of course, back then, she thought Charlie had loved her and Gabriel too. He treated them both like they were royalty. And she ate it up.

"I've asked you a million times not to stop by unannounced. It confuses Gabriel, especially when I have to ask you to leave."

"So, ask me to stay for dinner." He winked. "You know how much I love spending time with Gabriel. And you. I've missed you."

"We got divorced for a reason."

Charlie narrowed his stare. "If you recall, I didn't want that divorce and I was willing to do whatever it took, including counseling, which I'm still happy to do. That's also in part why I told my father I wanted to be the one to open our new offices here in Lighthouse Cove. I'm here. I'm fighting for us. You're the one who bailed."

She knew without a shadow of a doubt that Charlie had to be the one who came up with the idea to open an office here. But what really burned her ass was that this kind of town was not where Charlie wanted to live. He preferred to be where all the money and action was, and that was Palm Beach. Not almost an hour north, where the real estate was far less valuable and the entire vibe was small town and flip-flops, not high society and Chanel. Charlie would get bored with the clientele and what they could afford, not to mention the nightlife that ended at eleven.

If he couldn't hobnob with the rich and famous, it wasn't worth it to him, plain and simple.

"We're over. You need to get that through that thick skull of yours and let me and Gabriel go. That starts by easing yourself out of our lives again so Gabriel can adjust. I'm begging here."

"I've been in his life since your parents up and left you to care for him. He was ten years old." Charlie inched closer. "I gave you both a home. I took you in and I'm not the one who gave up on us. You did that."

"Oh, really." She clutched the side of her sofa. The one she bought at a secondhand store because Charlie was an asshole. Him and his damn prenup. Well, she didn't need his fucking money. She'd make it on her own. She didn't need his breadcrumbs and she wasn't about to take them. They always came with conditions anyway. "You're honestly going to stand there and forget about the time I found you—"

"Hey, Liberty, Miles is…" Gabriel came barreling through the front door of her three-bedroom home that she'd managed to purchase with her small divorce settlement. At least she'd managed to get something out of Charlie. Fucker. "Oh, hi, Charlie." Gabriel's eyes were wide and he didn't smile.

Gabriel had always been able to sense the tension in the air, and it affected him deeply.

She hated that for him.

"Hey there, buddy." Charlie wrapped his arm around Gabriel. "How are things going?"

"I didn't know you were coming today," Gabriel said.

For the first month they had lived in this house, Charlie had started to become a distant memory for Gabriel. It had been hard, since he'd been so attached to the man for years. However, Gabriel was a smart young man, and he'd been there on so many nights when Liberty sat in her room, crying. She'd tried to be quiet, but Gabriel still heard her and every once in a while, he came in to comfort his big sister.

He was good that way.

He knew Charlie had hurt her, but he believed one big whopper of a lie that Charlie had told, and that was the one wedge that existed between brother and sister that she'd never be able to fix because it meant telling Gabriel the truth. It would break his heart to learn of that kind of betrayal by another human in his life, and he'd been through enough. Not to mention that for Gabriel, every day was a struggle. He was neither high-functioning, nor low-functioning, but somewhere in the middle. He had a base level intelligence and could hold his own in conversations, if he felt comfortable. But that was the rub. He had few social skills and without her, he would never get along in this world.

"Charlie just came by to tell me something," Liberty said. "He was just leaving."

"Oh. Okay." Gabriel nodded.

Ever since Charlie rolled into town, Gabriel had flip-flopped between being glad to see him to not wanting to be around him at all. She didn't want to poison Gabriel's thoughts against Charlie. That wouldn't be right. And the therapist she spoke to told her it wouldn't help Gabriel adjust to his new environment anyway. It would only cause him stress. It was one of the reasons she waited for her divorce to become final before moving.

Making it all that much harder on herself.

But Gabriel's adjustment was more important.

"Um, Miles is outside," Gabriel said. "I told him I'd come get you because I didn't recognize the car in the driveway."

"That's because I just bought it. Isn't she pretty? I'd love to take you for a spin," Charlie said, giving Gabriel a squeeze.

Gabriel's eyes grew wide.

Fuck.

Gabriel loved cars. Had a passion for them and when Miles had offered him a job, it had been a godsend in more ways than one.

"Just a quick ride, and then I'll be on my way." Charlie smiled. "Promise."

"Please, Liberty. Can I go?" Gabriel asked. The man was twenty-two. It broke her fucking heart that he had to ask her permission. It didn't matter how smart he could be, his emotions were that of a toddler sometimes.

"Sure," she said. "But not too long. We have dinner and you have work bright and early."

"I'll have him back in a half hour." Charlie turned, his arm still looped around Gabriel's shoulders, and sauntered toward the front door.

She followed, stepping out onto the front porch.

"Hey, Miles." Gabriel waved. "I'm going for a ride in that," he said with excitement laced in every syllable. "It's a Porsche 911 GT3. Isn't it cool?"

"She sure is and she looks like she was just driven right off the showroom floor." Miles leaned against the big palm tree in the front yard. "Charlie." He nodded.

The two men had met in passing half a dozen times or so. While it had been cordial, it had never been completely pleasant. More like chest-pounding gorillas sitting in their corners, sizing each other up, waiting to pounce on one another.

"Miles, is it?" Charlie paused by the tree, looking Miles up and down, as he did with most people. And he sure as hell knew the man's name because he asked who he was and why he was stopping by all the damn fucking time. His words, not hers.

Charlie certainly didn't like that Gabriel was

working for Miles either. He thought Gabriel should come work with him, in fucking real estate. That was no job for Gabriel. He struggled with strangers. And even though he knew his way around a computer better than most, that man liked to tinker with cars. Miles said he was damn good too. A natural.

And it made Gabriel happy.

Especially when moving had put him in a funk, including some self-harm issues, but that had all changed when Miles came into the picture.

She wasn't sure what to make of that.

Or Miles.

And his odd charm. It was different from Charlie. More subtle and genuine. As if everything he said and did was just the way he was, no matter who he was talking to, man or woman.

"My name hasn't changed since five days ago," Miles said.

Liberty cringed. Pissing off Charlie wouldn't help her situation. It would only make matters worse.

Perhaps it was time to tell her sexy neighbor a few things.

Charlie pointed his key fob in the direction of his new toy. "Go ahead and get in the passenger side. But don't touch anything, okay, buddy?"

"Sure thing." Gabriel raced to the side of the sports car and climbed in.

Charlie inched closer to Miles.

Shit. This couldn't be good.

She flew down the steps two at a time, prepared to separate the two.

"I don't know who you think you are," Charlie said. "But that's my wife. I expect you to be gone when I get back." He turned on his heel and marched to the car, sliding behind the steering wheel and revving the engine before backing out of the driveway.

Miles pulled his phone out of his back pocket and tapped at the screen. "I suppose you heard that," he said without looking up.

"I did," she admitted. "Who are you texting?" Not that it was any of her business, but damn if she wasn't curious.

"I'm not sure you want me to give you an honest answer to that question." He stuffed his phone back in his jeans pocket.

She'd only known him for two months. The first time they'd met was the day she'd moved in and he'd helped unload the boxes from her U-Haul. She didn't have to tell him a single thing about Gabriel; he'd figured out all on his own that he needed to keep a safe distance and to let Gabriel dictate his own comfort level with Miles.

From there, Miles would be outside, sitting on his front step, with a football in hand. He'd wave, smile, and wait for Gabriel to interact.

Miles had a kind heart. She could see that from day one.

And he was damn fucking sexy with his thick, dark hair, intense blue eyes, and muscular frame.

As she navigated her way through town, she heard a few stories and Miles was a ladies' man. Full of charm. Definitely not the settling down type.

Not that she was looking.

"Now I have to know," she said.

"Chris Manzo, one of my mother's deputies."

"You didn't." She planted her hands on her hips. "You know my brother has issues with authority. If a cop pulls over Charlie, my little brother might freak out. That's the last thing I need."

"Relax. Chris won't pull him over with Gabriel in the vehicle. But if Charlie does anything remotely stupid, he will the second he leaves this house, without Gabriel in the car." Miles lowered his chin. "I wouldn't do that to Gabriel. You should know me better than that by now."

"The only thing I know right now is that you and I need to have a little chat." She grabbed him by his thick biceps and immediately wished she hadn't. Sparks flew from his skin through her fingertips and right to all her girly parts.

Not a sensation she welcomed.

She dropped her hand to her side as she made her way to the front steps and plopped down on the last two. "Why are you dressed in jeans and a T-shirt? I thought you were at your brother's wedding."

"I changed." He shrugged before planting his ass on her porch steps. "What has you so upset?"

"Many things, but only one that I'm going to discuss with you." She reached behind her head and tugged on her ponytail. "Look. I do really appreciate everything you've done for me. For Gabriel. You're so good with him and I value that. It's so nice to know that he's got a job that he's thriving in because…" She swiped at her eyes, fighting the tears. "…well, he's never been able to have one before. And it makes me having one that much easier."

Miles rested his hand on her knee and squeezed. "All he needs is a little understanding and for people not to freak out on him when he makes a mistake, which all of us do anyway. He's no different in that regard."

"Yeah, but most don't see it that way."

Damn Miles and his fucking understanding ways. She really resented his calm demeanor. It was as if nothing ever rattled the man.

"Did I do something wrong?" Miles asked. "Because if I did, I'd like to know what that was. My intentions are not to hurt him or you."

"That may be true, but you sure know how to get under my ex-husband's skin." She sighed.

He chuckled.

"It's not funny. All it serves is to make my life harder." She turned, catching his gaze. His damn sea-blue eyes sucked her right in.

If she were any other woman, she might fall for his charm.

"How so?" he asked, his hand still on her leg.

She should bat it away, but she didn't. It felt too nice. Too comforting. And that was dangerous. "It's not really any of your business, but I'm going to tell you anyway."

"Okay," he said softly. "I'm listening."

"My divorce was kind of ugly. Charlie didn't let me go easily. He comes from a rich and powerful family and I wanted out. I took a small settlement and once the divorce became final, I took Gabriel and moved up here. I thought that would be the end of it. But I should have known Charlie would be back. He doesn't like to lose. Why he still wants me, I have no idea. But he does. Your presence is making it more of a challenge for him. More like a game. It's compounded because of how Gabriel feels about you."

"Are you telling me that Charlie believes there's something going on with us?" Miles had the nerve to wink. And smile.

She poked him in the arm.

"Ouch. That hurt."

"It was supposed to," she mumbled. "You're making light of this situation and I don't appreciate it when I'm trying to be real."

"I'm sorry." He leaned back on his elbows, thankfully releasing her knee. "I'll be honest, I don't like your ex-husband and I certainly don't like some of the things Gabriel has told me about him."

She snapped up her head and shifted. "What? Gabriel has spoken to you about Charlie?"

"For the last two weeks, I've spent almost forty hours a week at the shop with Gabriel. We've chatted about a lot of things. Charlie is one of them." Miles sat up taller. "For the record, I'm not the one who brought up the topic, Gabriel did. All I did was listen."

"What did he say?" She couldn't believe it. Gabriel struggled to discuss any emotions. Even with her. They always came out sideways. When he got really upset, he often resorted to hitting his head with his fists. A few times he even threw things. It was why she had to keep her house so calm and why she put up with so much shit from Charlie in their marriage the last few years. Charlie had used it to keep her, something she never did understand, when it was obvious he didn't love her, not even one little bit.

He said he did, but the only thing that man loved more than himself was his money, power, and having his fill of other women.

That, she'd seen firsthand.

"I'd be breaking a confidence. His trust. And that's not something I'm willing to do to him as his friend and his boss," Miles said.

"Seriously?" She glared. "I'm his sister. His caretaker. The one person on this planet who loves him more than anything. I think I should know what he's thinking."

Miles reached out and tucked a piece of hair behind her ear. "I can see how much he means to you and what you do for him. I know you're only trying to protect him. I get that. I do. But trust me when I say that Gabriel is more than conflicted when it comes to Charlie. Gabriel has eyes. And ears. But he can't process and or distinguish between what Charlie does to you and how he treats Gabriel." Miles arched a brow.

"What the fuck are you implying?" Liberty had always had a bit of a truck driver mouth, something that Charlie and his family had tried to beat out of her. Charlie hated it. He wanted a lady. A woman to fit into his country club ways and for over ten years, she tried.

But it was like she was one of Cinderella's ugly stepsisters trying on the glass slipper. No matter how hard she tried, she just couldn't wedge her foot in that shoe.

And now it felt so good to just say every cuss word in the book.

"How dare you accuse me of not understanding my own brother. I practically raised him myself," she said.

Miles pressed his finger on her lips. "I didn't accuse you of any such thing."

"That's not what that sounded like to me." She pushed his hand away.

"Let me ask you this. Do you want Charlie in your life? In Gabriel's?" He lowered his chin. "And be honest with me because this is about you, not me. I can handle that either way."

"I divorced the man," she mumbled. "I believe it's obvious I don't want him around anymore. But with Gabriel, that's complicated. When he forms a bond with another human, ripping that away from him can cause problems. I have to be delicate in how I do that. You pushing Charlie's buttons is making it harder for me to ease that man out of our lives."

"Don't poke me again, but it's not me that's the problem. It's you."

She pursed her lips. "And why the hell do you say that?" she asked behind a tight jaw.

"Because you won't tell Charlie to fuck off. When he's around, you're all unicorn and rainbows in front of Gabriel. You act like it's okay for Charlie to waltz in and out whenever he wants. That's part of the confusion and in a nutshell, that's what has Gabriel questioning what's really going on."

She opened her mouth, but Miles silenced her with his damn fucking sexy finger again.

"Gabriel loves you. You're the one constant in his life and all he wants to do is please you. And yeah, he doesn't have the same emotions we do about people, but he's not dumb. He knows on his own level that

Charlie hurt you. I would bet the golf cart he and I have been working on that if you sat Gabriel down and let him know that you didn't want Charlie coming around anymore, he'd get through it. He has you to lean on and an entire community that has embraced him. I don't know a single person in Lighthouse Cove that has come across Gabriel who doesn't adore him or want to see him thrive here."

Well, fuck if she couldn't agree with that logic. Every time someone came into the Safe Harbor Café where she worked, they all raved about what an awesome human Gabriel was, making it easier for him to assimilate to his new surroundings.

It hadn't been like that in Palm Beach.

Not before she married Charlie.

And certainly not after.

Everyone always treated Gabriel differently.

But not here.

"I'm not saying I'm going to take your advice, but let's play hypotheticals here." She fiddled with her thumbnail. "If I tell Charlie never to come over again, not even if he calls first, what happens if he does? What do I do then? Or if he calls Gabriel. He does have his own phone."

"Simple." Miles yanked his cell from his back pocket. "You call one of my cop brothers and let them handle it. You file a formal complaint, it becomes harassment, and they will make him go away. I'm sending you their personal numbers. I'll let them know I did that," he said. "As far as Gabriel goes, just make it clear he needs to tell you and show you the messages. Then call one of my brothers. Emmerson or Emmett would be the best ones to reach out to."

"But isn't Emmerson the one who just got married? Won't he be going on a honeymoon?"

Miles shook his head. "Not for a couple of weeks, and maybe not even then. His wife has morning sickness."

"Oh. Well, too bad for the honeymoon, but congrats to the happy couple." She lifted her hand but immediately dropped it to her lap. She would not let the horror of losing her baby bubble to the surface. What happened had nearly destroyed her, but in the end, she had to accept that being tied to Charlie forever that way would have been the worst fucking hell.

"They are so ridiculously happy it's almost disgusting." Miles laughed, but it was cut short by the sound of a roaring engine.

Charlie.

"He's not going to be thrilled to see me," Miles muttered.

"Nope. He's not." She jumped to her feet. "Can you do me a favor and ask Gabriel to do something with you. Anything. If I don't talk to Charlie now, I might not have the nerve again."

"Happy to."

She turned. "One more thing. Gabriel might need a friend after I talk to him. Can you be available tonight after that?"

"Of course." Miles nodded.

"He could freak out. In that case, he won't be coming into work tomorrow."

"Whatever you and he need."

"Thank you." She smoothed down the front of her jean shorts. Time to take her life back.

## 3

"How was the car ride?" Liberty tried to pull Gabriel in for a hug. She took them when she could get them, and they weren't often. Gabriel wasn't one for physical touch and right now, he shied away.

That could mean a variety of things and she tried not to read anything into it.

"Fun," he said.

"Hey, Gabriel," Miles called. "Want to work on the golf cart with me?"

"Yeah." Gabriel took off running like a kid in a candy store, not bothering to say goodbye to Charlie.

Which was uncharacteristic, even for Gabriel.

She glanced over her shoulder and watched, her heart in her throat, as Miles and Gabriel strolled toward Miles' garage. Miles was so good at gauging Gabriel's emotions, or lack of them.

He knew when he could touch and when he couldn't.

And he understood this wasn't the time to even offer a squeeze of the shoulder.

"Did something happen?" She turned her attention back to Charlie.

"Nope." Charlie leaned against the sports car. "Who is that guy to you? Are you sleeping with him? I hope not."

"Even if I was, I'm not your wife, so that would be none of your business." She folded her arms. "We need to talk."

"I agree," Charlie said. "I've had enough of this little temper tantrum you've been throwing. I never should have signed those divorce papers. I thought if I gave you some space, you'd come to your senses, but this has gotten out of hand. It's time for you to come home. Where you belong."

She blinked. "Excuse me? Did you honestly believe I'd go through the trouble of divorcing only to take you back a few months later?"

"We went through a tough time. Perhaps we both needed space. Now it's time for us to reconnect."

"No, Charlie. It's time for you to leave me alone."

He pushed from his car and put his hands on her forearms. "Come on, babe. This is ridiculous. How long are you going to make me pay for one mistake?"

"One mistake?" She shrugged free. "Try a dozen and I'm not even going to get into that with you.

Come here one more time and I'm calling the cops. And don't even try to get to me through Gabriel. You need to stop contacting him. He's not your brother. He's nothing to you and stop acting like he is."

"I see that asshole over there has been putting ideas in your head. I know who his mother is."

"Miles, or his family, has nothing to do with this. I'm tired. I've tried playing nice. Not just for Gabriel, but because I saw no point in making a spectacle of what happened." She poked him dead center in the chest. Something she wouldn't have dared do in the past. "I did that for your parents and your father's business. I let everyone in Palm Beach believe I was the bitch who left you high and dry. I don't care that everyone still believes that. You can go back to your nice cushy life and leave me the fuck alone."

"I see your foul language has come back."

"It never fucking left me." She pointed to his car. "Now leave, or I call the cops tonight. Your choice."

Charlie leaned closer. "You're making a mistake."

"The only mistake I ever made was not doing this sooner." Damn, this felt way too good.

Charlie opened the driver's side door and smiled. "I give you a month tops before you're begging me to take you back." He climbed into his sports car and peeled out of the driveway.

"Never going to happen, asshole." She tugged at her ponytail and released her hair, letting it flow over her shoulders. She gave it a good shake, before turning on her heel and heading toward Miles' garage.

She owed him big-time for giving her the courage to do what deep down she knew she needed to. Dealing with Gabriel, however, might have to come in stages. She'd start slow, telling him some truths. She had to because Charlie wasn't going to be in their lives anymore and she owed it to her little brother to be honest.

Leaning against the opening of the garage, she smiled at the sight of her little brother leaning over the engine of the golf cart with a wrench in his hands and a towel over his shoulder.

"I know it's late, and the sun has already set, but are you boys hungry?" she asked.

"I'm starving." Gabriel stood. He looked so much like their father with his dark hair and blue eyes. But he'd gotten shortchanged in the height department. Their dad had been six-three and Gabriel only stood five foot ten.

Liberty took after their mother with her long blond hair, but she also had blue eyes. Height-wise, she was only five-five, whereas their mother had been five-seven.

She often wondered where in the world her parents ended up after they left Palm Beach, shamed for having a son with such a disability.

Assholes.

They didn't deserve to be parents of such a special man.

Her heart tightened. At one time, her father had a soft spot for Gabriel. Or at the very least, he would spend time with the boy. He would play games at night while he waited for his wife to get ready for whatever party they were going to attend that evening.

When she was ready, he'd stand up and tell his son he'd see him tomorrow and Gabriel would accept that small amount of attention from the man he called dad. But his mother wouldn't even acknowledge his existence, and that always did a number on Gabriel.

"Good, because I made your favorite," she said.

"Lasagna? With sausage?" Gabriel rocked back and forth, something he did when things troubled him.

Damn Charlie. What the hell had happened in that car ride?

"I sure did." She smiled. "What about you, Miles? Or did you fill up on wedding food?"

"I'd never turn down a home-cooked meal." He placed his screwdriver in the toolbox. One thing she noticed about Miles was he liked things neat. Organized. His auto shop was about the cleanest garage she'd ever seen. "But I don't want to intrude."

"You're not," she said. "Gabriel, go wash up. We'll be in shortly."

"Okay." Carefully, he placed his wrench where it belonged and scoffed off toward their home.

Miles sat on the hood of the golf cart and wiped his hands on a towel. "While I want to ask you how that went, I need to tell you something first."

"I don't like the sound of that."

"And I don't like breaking that man's confidence."

"It's interesting that you're always calling him a man when most call him a boy," she whispered, unsure of why she decided to call him out on that distinction.

"I've called him a boy before because he does have childlike qualities. But ultimately, he's twenty-two and that's a man. He deserves to be treated with dignity and respect." Miles ran his fingers through his thick, dark hair. "Gabriel said something a little disturbing while you were having your chat with Charlie."

"And what was that?"

"It appears that Charlie is digging for information about me." Miles lifted his hand. "That's not how Gabriel relayed the conversation. But some of the questions he was asking me I know he didn't come up with on his own. He pulled out his cell twice because he totally botched one of the things he was trying to ask me."

"Charlie thought we were fucking."

Miles pounded his chest and coughed. "That's not

quite how Gabriel put it, but yeah, that was one of them."

"What did you tell him?"

"The truth." Miles arched a brow. "That we were friends, but that I liked you and wouldn't mind taking you out."

"Fuck," she mumbled, planting her hands on her hips.

"I take it that I've just crashed and burned. Again."

She laughed. "You do know that I haven't had three seconds since my conversation with Charlie to talk to Gabriel, so he's probably inside right now texting Charlie that you're hot for me. Gabriel is a loyal human and right now, he still has some loyalty for Charlie."

"If it makes you feel any better, I asked him to keep that to himself because I wanted to ask you proper." Miles took out his cell and stared at the screen.

God, that pissed her off.

"Eyes up here," she said.

He glanced up. "Sorry."

"For the record, it doesn't. Like I said, Gabriel has a sense of loyalty and he's being put between a rock and a hard place. Not so much by you, but by that asshole of an ex-husband of mine. I wouldn't be surprised if he turns around and comes right back."

Miles waved his cell. "Right now, he's getting a

speeding ticket for doing fifty in a thirty-five by my mother and she's pissed."

"Wonderful. You pulled your mother out of her son's wedding just to piss off Charlie because you could."

Miles pushed from the golf cart and inched closer. "No. Actually, I didn't. My brother's wedding was broken up because there was a three-alarm fire outside of town that required Jameson and basically all hands on deck. That dick of an ex-husband cut her off and nearly caused an accident. My text to Chris had nothing to do with it because he was already at the scene."

"Oh."

"I don't have to come over for dinner if you'd rather have a conversation with Gabriel. But I didn't want you to go into it without knowing what Charlie was fishing for."

"I'm sorry," she whispered. "I shouldn't have laid into you that hard."

"It's okay. I get it. I know this isn't easy for you." He traced her jawline with his finger.

"How did you get to be so understanding about someone like Gabriel?" she asked with her breath stuck in the center of her chest.

"That's a story for another day." His lips were so close she could feel his hot breath tingle against her skin. His mouth covered hers in a sweet, tender kiss. It started slow, building with intense heat that crawled across her body like hot lava flowing from a volcano. It was the kind of kiss that promised all the passion and desire in the world.

It was a dangerous kiss and one she should end.

Along with this dance she was doing with Miles. They could be neighbors. And friends. But not this.

She fisted his shirt and pushed, blinking her eyes open.

He licked his lips and smiled.

Her heart tumbled like a bowling ball being hurled down an alley, preparing to hit every single pin for a strike. "Well, if you're hungry, I've got plenty. Maybe you can help me with Gabriel. He responds well to you and Lord knows he's going to need someone he can trust and he's going to be angry with me after I tell him Charlie's not going to be welcome anymore."

Shit. She was playing with fire and she was going to get burned.

***

Miles leaned back, raising his wineglass and taking a sip. He generally wasn't a wine guy, but he could appreciate the flavor and this particular red blend did go well with pasta. Not to mention the company. "That was delicious. Thank you." The dinner conversation had been light. Airy. Mostly the topic of discussion had either been the auto shop or the golf cart.

But Gabriel hadn't been his usual chatty self. He loved cars and he knew more about them than he was given credit for. He was a quick study, when someone took the time to try to figure out how he learned and processed information. His reading skills were better than Miles by a long shot, but Gabriel didn't take verbal instruction as well, and that had made it harder for Miles. They were opposite that way.

But they both thrived in an environment where they could learn by doing and once Gabriel got it, he retained it.

He was a hard worker. He wanted to please Miles and everyone in the shop. Gabriel had drive and determination.

Miles understood that kind of passion in a world that didn't make sense, and finding that singular place where you fit was hard.

Those days were long gone for Miles, but it didn't mean he didn't remember them well.

Liberty pushed her plate to the side and folded her hands on the kitchen table.

The setup of her house was almost identical to Miles' with an eat-in kitchen in the rear of the house, a family room in the front, and a master bedroom next to that. Then there were two bedrooms upstairs. The only real difference was that her house needed a ton of work. The hardwood floors were a mess, whereas he had refinished his. The walls needed a fresh coat of paint and the stairs squeaked.

All of that, he and his brother Jameson could easily fix.

The outside would take a little more work as all the windows needed to be replaced. Not only were they old, but they weren't hurricane grade. Jamison's contacts could get her a really great deal, and he'd like nothing more than to do that for her.

But one thing at a time.

"Gabriel, I need to talk to you about something important," Liberty said in a soft, tender tone, one that a mother would say to a small child, and for some reason that grated on Miles' nerves. It wasn't his place to step between these two siblings. He'd be pissed if someone did that to him and one of his brothers if they didn't truly understand the dynamics of the relationship.

However, Miles knew two things about Gabriel. One was that he was capable of more than anyone knew. Maybe even his sister, who tended to baby him, though with good reason.

The second was that he didn't process emotion the same way everyone else did and had to be guided. That wasn't something that Miles had much experience with.

"Okay." Gabriel continued to stare at his plate, pushing a few pieces of food around.

"It's a difficult topic and might be unsettling," Liberty continued.

"Are we moving again?" Gabriel jerked his head.

"No. No. Honey. It's not that. But I've made a hard decision. It involves you and I wanted to tell you. I thought having Miles here might help with the transition."

Oh boy. While Miles could understand the gentle touch and the kind, soft tone, he couldn't get behind the way she spoke to him. It was as if she were talking to a two-year-old, which he wasn't. But it all came back to Miles' lack of understanding how Gabriel dealt with his raw emotions. So, Miles would have to sit back and let this one play out for now.

Gabriel placed both hands on the table and rocked back and forth, as if he were preparing himself for the worst.

Miles had seen this behavior before at the shop, twice. The first time had been when a customer, who hadn't been made aware of Gabriel's special circumstances, became abrupt and spoke tersely. Miles had been terrified he was going to have to call Liberty at work, but he'd been quickly able to redirect Gabriel. It hadn't been that difficult to do, and he certainly didn't coddle the man. At least not with his tone or demeanor. He spoke to him the same way he would any other person. The only difference was he didn't expect Gabriel to just *get over it*. Miles knew that wasn't possible. Instead, he spent time under the hood with Gabriel until Gabriel calmed down to the point he could focus on something else. It had taken a good forty-five minutes.

But it was well worth it to see Gabriel excel and move past a trying situation.

Liberty rose, moved to the other side of the table, and sat down next to her brother, resting her hand over his, holding them and rubbing her fingers over his palms. "Gabriel. I didn't mean to frighten you. We just need to make a few changes and I know change can be hard for you."

Gabriel sucked in a deep breath and let it out slowly but didn't stop rocking. He kept his gaze on his water glass and didn't say a word.

"I've asked Charlie to stop coming around. He's not my husband and it's time for me to have a clean break." She leaned forward. "I'm sorry this affects you, but I can't have you spending time with him either. It's going to be an adjustment, but we have each other."

"You don't want me to see him or talk to him? Ever?" Gabriel asked.

"I know that's asking a lot, but yes. It's time for us to have a fresh start. Just the two of us," she said.

Gabriel's chest rose and fell with a huff. "I'm tired and want to go to bed."

"Is that all you have to say?" Liberty asked. "I know Charlie means a lot to you and I'm not—"

"I don't. Want. To. Talk. About it." Gabriel slammed his hands on the table and stood. He shoved his chair back so hard it fell over. He stomped off through the house and out the front door.

Liberty jumped to her feet and lunged forward. "Gabriel. Come back here."

Miles stepped in front of her, wrapping his arms around her tiny waist. "Let me go."

"You don't know how to handle him when he gets like this." She glared.

"Let me try."

"He's my little brother and he's… fine, but if he's self-harming, you have to promise to get me."

"I will." Miles squeezed her shoulder before leaning in and kissing her cheek, letting his lips linger longer than he should have, but he wanted her to know he was on her side as much as he was Gabriel's. He turned and made his way outside where he found Gabriel pacing across the front yard, tugging at his hair and calling himself names.

Damn, that broke his heart.

"Gabriel. Come sit with me." Miles took a seat on the last two steps of the porch.

"I. Don't. Want. To. Talk. About it." Gabriel gave his head a good pound.

Shit. "I don't either," Miles said. "And I'm not asking you to tell me anything. Just to come take a load off."

"Okay." Gabriel kicked the grass before stomping over, at least with his hands at his sides.

With a big huff, he fell back on the steps. "She treats me like a baby. I'm not a child. I'm a man."

"That you are." Miles leaned forward and rested

his elbows on his knees. "But are you angry because of how she talked to you or that she told Charlie not to come around anymore?"

"Both," Gabriel whispered in a small, childlike voice. "But I still don't want to talk about it."

"I can't force you to do that." Miles rubbed the back of his neck. "However, I'd like to give you some advice."

"What's that?"

"I think you should tell your sister that it bothers you when she babies you like that. Let her know that you understand she's only trying to protect your reactions, but that how she's doing it makes it worse. That you'd rather she just tell you."

"It makes me so angry. I get I'm different, but she knows how to really make me feel that way."

"She loves you and only wants what's best for you." Miles gave Gabriel a little punch in the arm. "You know, sometimes when we're different from others, the people who love us the most, in an attempt to protect us or make things easier for us or even to teach us the hard lessons in life, they do the dumbest things. Trust me, I know a little about that."

"You're not different. You're cool."

Miles burst out laughing. "I'm glad you think so, but growing up, I wasn't. I was the dumb kid. The one who all the other kids picked on." He tapped his temple. "Because I don't process information the way everyone else does."

"I don't know what that means."

"I have a couple learning disabilities that made school incredibly difficult. I had to repeat second grade, putting me in the same grade as my younger brother, Jameson. But it got worse. I flunked most of my classes my junior year and that meant I wasn't going to graduate with Jameson. Not only wasn't I down with that, but neither was my mother. Her approach was forcing me into summer school and tutors and drilling it into my head that I was going to be a big fat loser if I didn't get my shit together."

"Your mother said that to you?"

Miles cringed at the memory of the words his mom actually used. Twenty-odd years later, his mother looked at him very differently. And his learning disabilities. But back then, she honestly believed someone could wave a magic wand and they'd vanish. If it hadn't been for Nathan, Seth, and his dad, he'd surely have been a bum. They had been the ones to sit their mom down and get her to agree to let him go to trade school. Becoming a grease monkey had been the best thing that had ever happened to him because it had given him purpose.

He became good at something other than being the dumb kid.

"Pretty much," Miles said. "Honestly, my mom did mean well, even if it was misguided. She wanted me to be successful in life."

"But you own your own business."

Jesus, Gabriel was good for his ego.

"I do. However, it took me a long while to get there between the pressure my mom put on me and the fact I struggled with the way I learn. It wasn't easy. Sometimes it's still not."

Gabriel started rocking.

"You're not understanding, are you?"

He shook his head.

"Can you do me a favor and take in a few deep breaths? That always helps me relax."

Gabriel did as Miles asked. The rocking slowed, but it didn't go away.

Progress, that's all Miles could ask for.

"You know how you sometimes process emotions differently than your sister. Or me?"

Gabriel nodded.

"Well, it's like that for me with information. I struggle with reading. I'm dyslexic, among other things."

"I've never heard of that before."

"It's a big word to describe someone who sees words on the page different from everyone else. It's so bad for me, that it's easier for me to listen to a book. Or to learn by doing something rather than have to try to read it. My mother always believed that in time, I'd simply overcome it."

"Haven't you?" Gabriel glanced up.

"Nope. Letters and numbers are still all jumbled on the page. It's why I almost never deal with the money at the shop and why Trinity has to run the business side of things. It's why I never became a cop like my brothers because I would have never been able to pass the entrance exam. Add that to something called ADD and what a psychologist would describe as generalized social anxiety, I was lucky to go to trade school and learn how to tinker with cars."

"But you're so good at doing that. The best. And you're good with people." Gabriel blinked his big blue eyes. "You're so smart when it comes to all that."

"I had some good teachers who understood that I didn't process information the same way. But people. Not so much. I do well with one-on-one situations, but I hate crowds. Despise them," Miles said. "Your sister totally gets you and how you deal with emotions. I get that she doesn't always go about talking to you the right way, but cut her a little slack when it comes to Charlie. While she might not want him in her life and you need to respect that, she doesn't want to hurt you in the process."

"That does make sense." Gabriel sighed. "I'm tired. Do you mind if I go to bed now?"

"Not at all. I'll see you first thing in the morning for work." Miles held out his fist.

Gabriel pounded it.

Miles leaned back on his elbows and let out a long breath. While he got Gabriel to understand his sister meant well and that maybe a conversation might be in order, Miles still had no idea what had upset the man in the first place.

And it wasn't being spoken to like a child because it wasn't that bad. Not to mention that it was all in the tone because of his emotions. Change the tone, and he wouldn't feel like he was being treated differently.

But that was all beside the point.

Charlie had put Gabriel between a rock and a hard place and that was what had gotten Gabriel upset.

The floorboards rattled under his ass. He turned his head. "Hey," he said, staring at Liberty's sexy legs as she made her way down the steps.

He'd been instantly attracted to her from the moment he'd laid eyes on her two months ago. Lots of women turned his head, but not like Liberty and that was odd. He never went for women who had baggage and he could tell just by looking at her that she carried a few suitcases full.

For an entire month, he admired her from a distance while he got to know Gabriel. He sort of felt like a shithead for doing that. But then in walked her asshole ex-husband, reminding him of why he didn't do women with a checkered past.

Only, he couldn't keep his distance if he tried.

And he hadn't tried all that much.

"I owe you an apology." Liberty stretched out her legs.

"For what?"

"Eavesdropping." She smiled sheepishly.

He shook his head. "Didn't trust that I could calm him down?"

"Maybe."

"I've told you about every issue he's had at work." Slowly, he rose. "I said I wouldn't meddle. But fuck it. You've got to stop treating him like a child." He held up his hand. "Stop coddling him. He's been dealing with who he is for as long as you have. He's got some coping skills. Let him use them and when he's off the deep end, redirect."

"He's my brother." She raised her hands and slapped them on her legs. "I love him and I watched him cry for months after our parents abandoned him. And again after I told him Charlie and I were getting divorced. I hate hurting him this way. So excuse me if I want to ease that pain for him and absorb it on myself." She let out a long breath. "It's not that I didn't trust you. I wouldn't be sending him off to work with you if I didn't. There's an adult program one town over that deals with adults on the low end of the spectrum, but I know he's higher functioning than that and I didn't want to do that to him. It's what Charlie's family did and honestly, Gabriel hated it."

"Then why did you listen in on a private conversation?" Miles cocked his head.

"It started off as simply watching, but I became fascinated by how quickly you got Gabriel to sit with you. Not many people can do that. And then there was the conversation." She tucked her hair behind her ears. "I have to know. Was all that stuff true?"

"Jesus. You honestly think I'd make that up?" He raked his fingers through his hair. "Don't answer that. It's late and I'm tired. I'll see Gabriel at six for breakfast since I know you have the early shift." He spun on his heel and strolled across the yards to his home. He no longer had the bandwidth to deal with her, or his attraction to her, a second longer.

## 4

Liberty poured herself two fingers of bourbon and took it outside. She leaned against the porch railing and stared across the lawn.

Miles' home was so much nicer than hers with his new roof and siding, perfectly manicured lawn, and beautiful landscaping that he took care of himself. His grass was this picturesque green that belonged in a home and gardens magazine and all his bushes and trees were filled with bright colors that made her home look like one big turd, especially when she knew damn well the layout of both structures was almost identical.

Light filtered through the front windows of Miles' house. Those were the family room and possibly the master bedroom.

He was still awake.

Fuck it. She wasn't going to let this linger. She owed him an apology and dammit, she was going to give him one.

Tossing back her head, she downed a shot of courage. She set the tumbler on the small table and marched herself across the lawns, feeling the difference between her crunchy grass and his soft plush turf.

Lifting her hand, she pounded on the door.

It opened seconds later. Miles stood in the doorway wearing only his jeans, which weren't buttoned, and he was barefoot.

She swallowed. "Hi," she managed.

"What are you doing here, Liberty?"

"Can I come in? I won't stay long. Promise."

He took a step back and waved his arm. "Would you like a drink? I was just about to pour myself a nightcap."

"Sure, why not." She followed him back into the kitchen. "Wow. This is nice." She ran her fingers across the white and green granite countertop. "Did you do all this work yourself? Or did you hire someone?"

"Jameson and I did most of it. What was above our pay grade, we subbed out." Miles pulled down two short glasses and waved a bottle of tequila. "I'm in the mood for something different."

She nodded. "How long did it take you to finish this remodel?"

"I'm not done yet. The upstairs is a mess and right now, my master shower is out of commission." He handed her a tumbler and leaned against the counter. "I don't mean to be rude, but it's late and I was going to have this one shot and go to bed, so what's on your mind?"

"I see you're still pretty pissed at me."

He ran his hand over his mouth. "I'm not sure that's the right emotion. It might be coming out sideways."

"I'm sorry I implied you could be fibbing to my brother." She tossed her shot back and inched closer. She curled her fingers over his thick biceps. A shock raced through her system like a lightning bolt. Her fingers stuck to his skin like hot glue. "People do it all the time and generally, they mean well, but if Gabriel learns the truth, it always ends up a mess."

"Once again, proof he's not that much different than the rest of us, because that would anger me too." He reached out and tucked a few pieces of her hair behind her ear. His touch was tender. Gentle. Kind.

"I didn't mean to insult you in my desire to protect my brother from more hurt and pain. I know you care about him and to be honest, I was both touched and little surprised by your big reveal to Gabriel. You're incredibly sensitive to others and you're one of the smartest people I know."

He cocked his head. "I might give you the former, but not so much the latter." He laughed. "Ever wonder why I listen to my texts most of the time over reading them?"

"No." She shook her head. "And that has nothing to do with one's intelligence." Gently, she poked his chest, for no other reason than she wanted to touch his body. "Everyone in this town says you know more about cars than anyone else. I've heard from a few people that you're pretty good with historical facts too."

"Rote memorization is what got me through school. Doesn't make me smart." He folded his arms.

Damn, he honestly believed he wasn't intelligent.

That tore through her soul.

She rested her hand on his shoulder, leaned in, and pressed her lips against his cheek, letting them linger longer than she should. "Thank you for all that you do for Gabriel and please accept my apology for being a bitch."

"You're welcome and it's forgotten." He grabbed her wrist. "But don't ever call yourself that again. Now that we've talked, I understand why you thought I might have done that. Just in the future, lead with stuff like that."

"I can do that."

"Good."

Her chest heaved up and down with every deep breath. She stared into his eyes and his captivating gaze wouldn't let her look away. Her attraction to him confused her and she didn't know how to contain it any longer. Desire and passion rippled across her skin like a rudder cutting through the water.

He took her chin with his thumb and forefinger, parting her lips. A moan escaped her throat, and his mouth covered hers in one of the most electrifying kisses she'd ever experienced.

Not that she'd had many.

She'd started dating Charlie when she'd been twenty and he'd been twenty-six. She suspected Miles had closer to ten years on her, but with him, it didn't feel the same way. With Charlie, there had always been this odd parent-child relationship. He never treated her like an equal.

Miles did.

Slowly, his hand glided down her neck, landing on her breast. His touch was soft, barely a caress, until his thumb grazed her taut nipple.

Arching her back, she dug her fingers into his skin while he teased and tortured her body relentlessly.

Gloriously.

He lowered his head and drew her nipple into this mouth through her clothing as he grabbed the back of her legs, hoisting her up onto the counter.

She curled her fingers over the island's edge and stared at him as he tore off her shirt and dropped her bra to the floor. She opened her mouth, but no words came out. His fingers and tongue explored her breasts and the rest of her body exploded like a rocket ship hurling its way toward space.

Kissing his way down her belly, he quickly undid her jean shorts. Before she could suck in a deep breath, those were thrown across the room and two of his fingers were thrust deep inside while his tongue danced wildly over one nipple and then the other.

"Liberty, do you want me to stop?" Miles whispered.

"No," she managed.

He continued to stoke her insides, rubbing his thumb over her throbbing clit with soft, expert strokes. He stared into her eyes, increasing the pressure, and adding a finger. "Let go for me, Liberty."

She trembled, her breaths coming in shallow, gasping bursts. She couldn't believe how quickly she had surrendered to Miles' expert touch. She knew she was close, her climax building with each caress.

"Let go, Liberty," he whispered again, his voice low and gravelly. His eyes locked on hers, demanding and desperate, needy and raw.

And just like that, Liberty shattered. With a loud, keening cry, she released her control, her body convulsing and shaking.

"That was amazing." Miles kissed her cheek. Her neck. He traced his wet fingers up her belly, around her nipple, and then licked them with a wicked smile. "Just like honey."

She was putty in his hands and he'd rendered her absolutely speechless.

He took a step back, yanked his wallet from his

back pocket, and pulled out a condom, setting it on the counter. "We can end this here, if you'd like."

She swallowed. "No. I want more." She slid her hand inside his jeans.

Miles' smile grew wider as she reached for him. He helped her pull his jeans down, revealing his taut, muscular form. As he stood before her, naked and ready, a sense of awe washed over Liberty. This moment, this connection, it was unlike anything she had ever experienced.

With trembling hands, she wrapped her fingers around him, feeling the familiar yet overwhelming sensation of his hardness in her palm. As she ran her hand over his length, his eyes never left her face. He kissed her deeply. Passionately. The intensity of the moment left her breathless, and her heart raced in anticipation of what was to come.

He eased back onto the kitchen chair, tearing open the condom and covering himself.

She climbed onto his lap, gripping his shoulders and taking him slowly until he rolled his hips, each movement eliciting a new wave of pleasure.

Their bodies seemed to align perfectly, as if the universe had conspired to bring them together. Liberty felt the sweat on their skin meld into one, their hearts beating in sync with each other's. She gazed into his eyes, seeing a world of love and lust, promise and desperation.

His hands gripped her hips, guiding her as she

rode him. His breaths came in short, sharp gasps. Liberty felt the rhythm of their lovemaking intensify, the urgency and the tenderness of it all blending together in a perfect symphony of pleasure.

As Miles watched her, she could see a mix of emotions flit across his face—desire, tenderness, and something… something she couldn't quite put a name to. It heightened her senses, making every touch more intense, every kiss more passionate.

The heat between them was palpable. Their bodies glistened with sweat and desire. Liberty's movements became more frantic, her breaths shallow and ragged. Miles' grip on her hips tightened. The rhythm of their bodies reached a crescendo, and Liberty felt as though she were flying, her world narrowing down to the two of them in this moment.

As the climax approached, a wave of euphoria surged through her system. She leaned in to kiss him, their tongues intertwining in a passionate embrace. Her orgasm exploded like the final few moments of fireworks on the Fourth of July. It was followed by Miles' release, which tingled her insides, giving her another mini climax.

He wrapped his arms around her like a warm blanket as she did her best to catch her breath. It was a perfect mix of wild abandon, and something a little more.

He kissed her neck and ran his fingers up and

down her back. It was so soft and tender. As if this was more than a fleeting moment.

A hookup.

Sex in the kitchen.

She froze. What the hell had she done?

He jerked his head back and cupped her chin. "Regrets already?"

She mustered up her best smile because there was no way she could honestly have any shame about what just happened. But it would be hard to move past it. "No." She cupped his cheek. "I was simply brought back to reality and Gabriel wasn't asleep when I left."

"Ah. I see." He kissed her softly. "I take it you want to go in case he's looking for you or worried."

"I never told him I was coming over here and I didn't bring my phone. I'm sorry. It's not like I want to rush off." She suddenly became very aware she was naked, straddling him at his kitchen table.

"I get it." He kissed her nose. "But I really don't like your running out of here like this. I'd like to see you tomorrow. Actually, I'd like to take you out, proper and all."

"We can talk about it later." She kissed his sweet lips. There was no way she would get into a relationship with Miles. No matter how much she liked him, it would never work. Besides, there were too many things in her life she needed to work on.

## 5

"Thanks for coming over so early." Miles handed his brother Rhett a steaming mug of coffee.

"I had a bunch of errands to run in town anyway." Rhett stretched his legs and leaned back in the chair on the front porch.

Miles chose to lean against the railing so he could have a better view of Liberty's place.

The sun had yet to peek out from the horizon, but the glow of morning had started to erase the darkness of night.

"What's on your mind?" Rhett asked.

"I need a favor."

"All right." Rhett sipped his coffee. "I'm all ears."

"I want you to look into Charlie Livingston."

Rhett shook his head. "Man, you can do that yourself; you don't need me for that."

"I'm well aware that I could, but we both know it requires me to do a little extra on the reading end. I can't do research at work with her little brother standing over my shoulder while I'm constantly doing text to speech or asking someone to read it to me. And let's just say she's been in my house and I'm not going to prevent that from happening again."

Rhett's right brow shot up. "You slept with her."

"Don't make it sound dirty."

"I didn't. You're always the one who does that. All I did was state a fact." Rhett set his mug on the table, snagged his ponytail holder, and put his manly hair in that bun thing. He was the only one in the family who could pull off long hair and a beard, though he didn't dare grow one. His wife would shave it off in his sleep. "Why am I looking into her ex-husband?"

"Because I don't trust the man or why he's coming around. I want to know why he's moved here. The real reason. And why they got divorced."

Rhett leaned forward. "That, my little brother, is sketchy as fuck. You should be asking her that question, not digging in her background."

"Come on, man. We didn't give Emmerson this lecture when we went poking around in Rumor's life."

"You can't compare the two, and you know it."

"Are you going to do it or not?" Miles rubbed the back of his neck. The lights in the family room over at Liberty's house flicked on. A shadow eased across the window.

"Of course I am, but I'm also always going to tell you what I think and this time, I believe you're making a mistake. Before I come back with whatever I find, talk to her. Ask her. Especially if you want this one to last." Rhett smiled like the day his first kid was born.

"You can wipe that grin off your face. Cupid hasn't struck me down."

"Oh, he's got his arrow pulled back and aimed right for you. I don't think you're getting away this time." Rhett gave Miles a little jab in the arm. "I better get going. I'll be in touch as soon as I know anything."

"Thanks. I appreciate it," Miles said.

"Miles!" Gabriel barreled through the front door of Liberty's house wearing a T-shirt and a pair of SpongeBob Squarepants boxers.

"My wife made me get rid of all my cartoon boxers. It was a sad day in my house when that happened." Rhett shook his head. "I miss them."

"There's something seriously fucking wrong with you, dude." Miles smiled and waved. "Hey, Gabriel. What's happening this morning?" He raised his mug and sipped.

"Oh, hi, Rhett," Gabriel said. "Liberty's making waffles. Do either of you want some?"

"Does your sister know you're asking us?" Miles downed the last of his coffee and set it aside. It wouldn't be the first time Gabriel had invited him over without Liberty knowing anything about it. The first time, Liberty had been flustered, but she welcomed Miles. The second time, she took Miles aside and asked him to make sure Gabriel had permission before showing up.

It felt like he'd been back in middle school and his mother had scolded him for having friends over after school without asking first.

But he did understand.

Gabriel rubbed the side of his head and swayed side to side. "Um, well, no."

"Why don't you go ask her if it's okay and if it is, I'm down for some food," Miles said.

"But not me." Rhett waved his hand over his head. "Sorry, buddy. I've got to get going. Maybe next time."

"Okay." Gabriel turned and raced inside the house.

"That man cracks me up." Rhett slapped Miles on the back. "One second he's like a toddler. The next second he's schooling me on engines."

"He's taken to the profession with ease." Miles puffed out his chest like a proud father. He'd taken in a few apprentices over the years, knowing full well that if he trained them right, he ran the risk of them leaving his shop. The first one was still with him; the second one opened his own place three towns over. Miles couldn't blame the man if he tried. He'd done exactly the same thing to his mentor.

Gabriel stuck his head out the door. "She said it's fine. Come on over. Coffee is brewing." He disappeared back inside.

"Looks like you got a breakfast date." Rhett gave Miles a little jab in the biceps. "I'll catch you later." Rhett jogged down the steps and strolled toward his fancy oversized SUV.

Miles took his mug and made his way across the lawn. He hadn't liked how she slinked out of his kitchen last night. While he couldn't regret what happened, he did wonder if she did.

He opened the door and his nostrils were assaulted with the rich scents of sizzling bacon and bitter coffee. It reminded him of his childhood. His father always cooked a big breakfast. It was often the only time the entire family was around for a meal, even his mother, though she would often eat hers quickly and run out the door.

Or if she'd been working the night shift, she'd scarf it down and go to bed, while everyone else made plans for the day.

It wasn't that his mother hadn't been present in his life, she had been. And she'd been a kind and caring parent. But her career was her top priority and all seven boys felt that to their core.

"Want a refill?" Liberty lifted a pot of fresh brew and smiled weakly. Her cheeks flushed when their gazes locked.

"Thanks." He held out his mug while she poured. "Did you sleep well?"

She tilted her head and blinked. "Um, yeah."

He glanced over his shoulder.

Gabriel sat at the island, his attention on his iPad while he played some game. The man loved his games. When he had a break at the shop, he'd sit in Miles' office, devour his lunch, and then spend the rest of the time on the computer until Miles called him back to work.

Miles set his cup on the counter and rested his hand on Liberty's hip. "Are you okay?" He leaned closer and brushed his lips over her sweet mouth.

She jerked, taking a step back. "I'm fine," she said with a raised brow.

He might not always be the sharpest tool in the shed, but he could take subtle hints. This conversation would have to wait. "It smells delicious."

"Bacon is just about done, and the waffles are staying warm in the oven."

"I didn't think I was that hungry, but now I'm starving."

"Why don't you take a seat next to Gabriel. I'll serve it right up." She patted his shoulder.

He took his coffee and eased onto the stool. "What are you playing?" He leaned over Gabriel's shoulder and frowned as Gabriel quickly closed out the text messaging app.

Fucking Charlie.

"Just some solitaire," Gabriel said, pushing his tablet aside.

Liberty placed two plates on the counter. "Eat up, boys."

"This looks amazing." Miles dug right into the waffles, which were doused in syrup and topped with a little powdered sugar. The presentation was as if he were at a fine restaurant. And the taste was even better.

He picked up a slice of crispy bacon. "Oh, my. Do you cook like this every morning?"

Liberty laughed. "Twice a week. Otherwise, it's cereal or oatmeal."

"I get to choose which days. So once during the week and once on weekends," Gabriel said. "And once a week we go out for breakfast. It's my favorite meal. I could eat breakfast food all day long."

"I could too, but I do like a good hamburger and fries." Miles watched as Gabriel stuffed his face, barely even tasting his food, he ate it so fast.

Once Gabriel was done, he hopped off the stool. "I have to go shower for work." He marched off toward the stairs without another word, leaving him alone with Liberty.

Miles leaned back, sipping his coffee. He'd spent a good hour this morning lying in bed, going over everything he wanted to say to her, but now that he had her alone, the silence was deafening and no words filled his mind. She deserved a man who was whole. A man who could give her everything, and Miles was broken. He might have some skills and when he did that deep soul-searching that one therapist had him do occasionally, he could even tell himself he was a successful man.

But Miles was also a realistic person. He knew his limitations. He'd been living with them his whole life and there was no way in hell he could have accomplished anything in life without the support and help of his brothers.

And now his sisters-in-law.

Balancing his checkbook was beyond a struggle. It was impossible. It went beyond transposing numbers. He didn't have the kind of dyslexia where he could retrain his brain to see things properly. Words would always be jumbled. Sure, he could read. A little. But if he was ever to take a test, he needed someone to read him the questions.

The embarrassment and shame he'd felt his entire life still lingered. It didn't matter that he'd accepted who he was and could lean on family. It still often made him feel like less of a man.

Trixi's father had drove that point home.

However, none of that changed the emotions swirling in his heart or the pull Liberty had over his soul. It went beyond wanting to be with her again physically, because once surely wasn't enough. He wasn't sure now that he'd had a taste, he'd ever be able to get her out of his blood. Every time he closed his eyes last night, she entered his dreams. And when he blinked them open, she was the first thing that popped into his thoughts.

This was more than attraction.

Rhett and his damn fucking Cupid analogy.

He set his coffee on the counter and strolled around the island, taking her into his arms. There was no point in denying what he wanted. If she didn't want him, he could accept that. But there was only one way to find out.

"What do you think you're doing?"

"I was going to kiss you," he said. "And I'd like to know how you feel about last night and going out on a proper date with me."

Her lips parted and he took that as an invitation.

He pressed his mouth over hers, dipping his tongue inside.

A soft moan bubbled from her throat to his, encouraging him to deepen the kiss. Her nails dug into his shoulder blades for a brief moment before she ended the encounter.

"I don't want my brother walking in on this," she whispered, dropping her hands to her sides.

"He's in the shower."

"Not the point." She pushed from his embrace and gathered the plates, setting them in the sink. "Change is hard for him, and this would be one whopper of a new thing for him. I can't just have him find out by chance. He has to be eased into the concept."

"Does that mean you'll go out with me?" His lips curled into a smile, even though he tried like hell not to. He wiped his hand over his mouth.

"I don't know. With everything that's going on with Charlie, it might be too much for Gabriel right now. Maybe when things calm down."

Miles cocked his head. "Do you regret coming over last night? What happened between us?" There had only been one other time in Miles' life that he'd ever asked that question. The women he dated he never saw himself being with long term, except one. And even Trixi he wasn't sure about. To this day, he had no idea if he loved her or not. He had strong feelings for her and liked her more than most. But her being with him had come at a high price. Not so much for Miles, but Trixi stood to lose everything, including her family.

"No, Miles. I don't regret last night. I'm just not sure it can happen again. At least not right now. I'm sorry. It's not that I don't like you because I think it's fairly obvious that I do. Please understand that this has nothing to do with you or even me. My little brother is all I have in this world. He matters to me more than anything. His well-being is all that I care about. I first need him to adjust to not having Charlie in his life. Once I know Gabriel has accepted that, then and only then can I consider dating."

"First, I don't think you give Gabriel enough credit." He held up his hand. "I'll respect your decision. I'm not going to hound you about it. But I'm not going to give up either." Wow. Did that just come out of his mouth? When a woman brushed him off like that, he usually shrugged his shoulders and moved on.

But not with Liberty.

Even though part of him believed he should. It all came back to the same tired old tape.

He wasn't good enough and she knew it.

But his father once told him that unless a girl flat-out admitted that's why she didn't want him, then it was all in his head.

"Second, you should know that Gabriel was texting with Charlie." He pointed to the tablet on the counter. "I saw it when I sat down for breakfast."

"I'm not surprised." She sighed. "The only real question I have is whether Gabriel reached out or Charlie. My guess would be Charlie. Even though I upset Gabriel by telling him Charlie wouldn't be welcome anymore, he stopped texting him when we first moved here, except when Charlie texted him first."

"Does he ever tell you what they talk about?"

"Sometimes." Liberty nodded. "I'll talk to him about it later."

"I'm happy to have a chat with him at work. He jibber-jabbers all day anyway about all sorts of stuff.

Maybe he'll open up to me." Miles downed the last of his coffee.

"Don't press him." She reached out and curled her fingers around his biceps. "The last thing I need is for him to have an issue with you and not want to work."

"I hear you." He took a chance and stole a brief but powerful kiss, letting his lips linger on her mouth, rendering her speechless. He smiled. "Tell Gabriel to meet me by my truck in fifteen." He turned on his heel and made a beeline for the door with his heart hammering in his chest.

She might not have said yes.

But she sure as shit didn't say no.

And he did his best to push that beat-up old tape out of his mind.

---

Liberty sat in the break room at the Safe Harbor Café, stabbing her fork into her summer salad and pushing the food around. She'd barely slept all night, thanks to what most would refer to as a little booty call. Damn, she couldn't believe she'd slept with Miles.

She laughed at the thought. No. She more or less fucked him good. Or maybe it was the other way around.

She'd gone to see him only because she wanted to apologize and set the record straight.

Not end up screwing him right there in his kitchen.

It resolved nothing. She felt like crap over the way she'd dealt with Gabriel and her raging conflicting emotions regarding Miles, and she hadn't been able to settle her mind.

Of course, the texts from Charlie hadn't helped.

Fucker.

The man had made her life a living hell and he wasn't going to stop anytime soon.

Her only hope was that if she ignored him, he'd go away.

Only he went from calling her a selfish lying bitch to telling her he loved her, that he was sorry, and he wanted her back.

"You look like you swallowed a lemon." Lucy Ann, her boss and the owner of the café, strolled into the break room and plopped herself in the chair across from Liberty. "I hope it's not the change in schedule that's got you looking so down."

"Not at all. I have no problem working mornings and lunches. I just can't believe that Rumor is coming back tomorrow. She just got married yesterday." Liberty relished the idea of chatting about anything other than Miles or her ex-husband.

Lucy Ann laughed. "That's her and Emmerson for you. To them, each day is either just another day or a day to be grateful, depending on how you flip the coin."

"I wish I could look at life that way sometimes." Liberty pushed her salad to the side and lifted her iced tea, taking a big gulp. "I wanted this town to represent new beginnings for me and Gabriel. We've never lived anywhere other than Palm Beach and honestly, I hated it there."

"You don't seem to be the kind of girl who would get along too well in that town." Lucy Ann arched a brow.

Liberty laughed. "You don't know the half of it."

Lucy Ann glanced at her watch. "You've still got twenty minutes on your break. Why don't you tell me about it."

"It would take a lot longer than that." Since Liberty had been in Lighthouse Cove, she'd done her best to make the transition easy for Gabriel. Making friends wasn't something that came naturally for either her or her brother. Back in Palm Beach, she didn't really have friends. She only associated with those whom Charlie deemed acceptable, and those weren't the kind of people whom Liberty felt comfortable with, not even when she'd lived with her parents.

Liberty had rebelled against being rich. Sure, it came with many perks, one of them not having to worry if she could afford some of Gabriel's favorite foods, hence the breakfast schedule. And dinner schedule. She had to budget or she'd be broke.

Gabriel didn't understand that and she didn't want to place that burden on his shoulders, though he did insist on giving her part of his paycheck for rent. That made him feel like an adult, and she wouldn't take that away from him.

Her parents—well, mostly her mom—had made it clear that associating with people beneath their station in life might as well be a federal offense. Her mother hated the few friends she had because they weren't in the proper social circle. She never did understand that concept because half of the people who were deemed acceptable, were the types of people who looked down on everyone else.

She wasn't that person.

Since she moved to Lighthouse Cove, she'd met a few people she could call friends. People who didn't judge solely based on someone's bank account.

Lucy Ann.

Just about every female married to a Kirby.

And Miles.

Although, sleeping with Miles had complicated the hell out of that friendship. The sex had been right out of an erotic novel. She hadn't experienced anything quite like it before and she couldn't stop thinking about it if she tried.

"If you don't want to talk about it, that's fine. But I have to admit I'm more than curious about Palm Beach. Phil and I have gone down there a couple of times. We've done the window-shopping thing, because no way would I spend that kind of money on shit I could buy for half the price. We once went to that fancy hotel with all the restaurants, but only had one drink at the seafood bar. It was seventy-five dollars." Lucy Ann smacked her forehead. "And it wasn't half as good as what my husband makes here in this cheap-ass diner."

Liberty laughed. "Everything in Palm Beach is overpriced. You're not paying for the food or beverage; it's all about the experience. About being seen in the right place with the right people. It's honestly about the dumbest thing ever."

"You're telling me."

"I was born and raised there," Liberty said. "Oddly enough, my parents were loaded. And I mean, Palm Beach loaded." She couldn't believe she was telling anyone this story. Everyone in Palm Beach knew her past, but no one here did. However, all they needed to do was google her and they'd figure it out, so what the hell was the difference.

"Seriously?" Lucy Ann leaned forward, resting her chin in her palm. "Where are your parents now?"

"I honestly have no idea and couldn't care less. They left me to take care of my brother when I was twenty and he was just shy of eleven. And they took their millions with them."

"Ouch. That's not nice. Why did they do that?"

"The stigma of having a child like Gabriel," Liberty said, biting back the tears that were always threatening to break free when she allowed herself to think too hard about what her parents had done to both of them. She didn't have any regrets or resentments about dropping out of college to step in and take care of Gabriel.

But she did hate her fucking parents for it.

Especially her father. He'd at least been present in their lives. Shown some interest in what they were doing. He'd even asked her about college and what she wanted to do, as if he didn't agree with his wife's goals about finding her a suitable man to take care of her and give her the proper status in life.

She'd always believed her dad had been on her side. That he at least cared about her and Gabriel.

But he left anyway.

"What the hell is wrong with Gabriel? I mean, I get he's on the spectrum, or whatever they are labeling it these days, but he's a human. His shit stinks like the rest of us."

Liberty burst out laughing. Lucy Ann was a breath of fresh air. Hell, everyone in this sleepy little town made Liberty feel like there wasn't a damn thing wrong with either one of them and sometimes she wasn't sure how to deal with that. Charlie's parents tiptoed around Gabriel. They tolerated him, only taking him out in public when it suited their needs. Showing off the *special needs* kid to make them look better, as if they had a fucking heart.

And Charlie. At first, he acted like Gabriel was his

best friend. He used Gabriel to get to her, but she still didn't understand why. She was the poor waitress at the fine dining restaurant whom everyone pitied.

Lucy Ann reached across the table. "I'm sorry your parents did that to you. And to Gabriel."

"Gabriel is my whole world and I wasn't sure how I was going to manage it all. Enter my dick of an ex-husband. I knew who his family was and even him, even though he's about six years older than me. Our parents had yachts at the same marina. I remember him being popular. Stunningly handsome. And every girl wanted him."

"Except you?"

"Well, I am younger and was too busy trying to help Gabriel feel like someone cared because my parents hid him away. Once he was diagnosed, it was like they erased him. They didn't want anyone to know they had a dumb kid with the emotional band-width of a toddler, especially my mother. When I went to college, it was local and I lived at home. All my mother wanted me to do was get married to some guy like Charlie. I honestly never wanted that life. I figured I'd get a degree, save up some money, move away, and take Gabriel with me. But that didn't happen and I was struggling. Charlie offered me an out." Her phone buzzed in her purse. "Do you mind if I see who that is?" It was rare that anyone texted her. Lately, it was either Charlie—or Miles.

If it was Charlie, she was going to have to respond

and tell him to stop or she would have to take matters to the next level. If she dared.

"By all means."

Liberty dug into her bag and lifted her cell. "Shit. It's Miles and there's an issue at the shop." She stood. "I'm sorry, but I have to go. I know that leaves you—"

"I'll deal with it. Just let me know if you can come back or not." Lucy Ann rose and took her by the arms, pulling her in for a hug. "When you work for me, you become family. Remember that."

"Thank you." She fumbled with her phone, her fingers barely able to hit the screen.

**Liberty:** *I'll be right there. Walking. It will be faster.*

**Miles:** *I'll meet you at the corner.*

What the fuck? Where was Gabriel? No time to text back. She raced out the door and down the street. Miles' auto shop was only two blocks away. She came to the light at the center of town. It was red, but there were no cars, so she ran across the street.

Miles waved as he rounded the corner.

"Why did you leave Gabriel alone with Charlie?" she asked, trying to catch her breath.

"I didn't." Miles kissed her cheek and placed his hand on the center of her back as they walked the last block. "He's going for a joy ride with Emmett in his patrol car."

She skidded to a stop and glared at Miles. While she'd mentioned Gabriel struggled with authority, she hadn't said why. "Being in a police car is going to freak him out and he doesn't know your brother that well."

"I wouldn't have sent him if he didn't want to go, but he was excited."

"I find that hard to believe," she mumbled. "How did you get him away from Charlie?"

"He doesn't even know Charlie's here." Miles ran his fingers through his thick, dark hair. "I was out back talking with Emmett when I saw the Porsche coming. I called for Gabriel and asked him if he wanted to go for a ride with Emmett. He jumped at the chance. They might go see Emmerson and Rumor. I told Emmett not to come back until I texted him."

"I think Gabriel has a bit of a crush on Rumor." She squared her shoulders as the body shop came into sight.

"Doesn't everyone?"

She chuckled. "That's your sister-in-law."

"And my brother's a lucky man." Miles turned his head and winked.

"If you're trying to settle my nerves, it's working."

"Good." He tugged her tighter and kissed her temple. "Just so you know, Charlie says he's here to have me service his car."

"It's brand new. Why would he need that?"

"He told me he wants to take it on the racetrack, but he needs two thousand miles on it first. He's only got three hundred. I told him to bring it back when he hits the right mileage and I'll certify it, but that didn't satisfy him. He asked about Gabriel and I told him he was out for lunch. I believe he's waiting for him to return." Miles pointed toward Charlie, who leaned against his precious Porsche. It wasn't the first one he owned, and it probably wouldn't be the last.

She paused on the sidewalk and turned. "I think I need one of your brother's or maybe your mother's help."

"With what?"

"This." She pulled out her cell and pulled up the text string from last night and this morning. "I want him out of my life. And Gabriel's. For good this time."

Miles took the phone and scrolled through the messages. He didn't arch a brow or show any emotion at all. "Emmerson went through something similar with his ex. I'll text my mom to come down. She'll document this. Unfortunately, for now, that's all we can do. Until she gets here, I don't want you saying too much. And I certainly don't want you getting into an argument with him. Save it for when she gets here."

"This isn't going to go over well." She turned, sucking in a deep breath, and rubbed her hands down her jeans.

"It never does." Miles looped his arm around her waist, guiding her across the pavement.

"Hey, babe." Charlie smiled. "Where's Gabriel? I thought I'd take him to lunch."

"He had plans," she said. "And stop calling me that."

Charlie narrowed his stare, glancing between her and Miles, whose arm was firmly planted around her body.

Part of her wanted to push Miles away. It only served to piss Charlie off even more. But maybe that's all she needed to drive the point home. Charlie could have almost any woman he wanted in Palm Beach. They were lining up at the door when she walked out. Hell, they were doing that before she left. It didn't matter that most only wanted his money. And if they had family money of their own, they wanted his family name.

Livingston.

Something she dropped the day she got divorced.

While she didn't like the name Blue, and all that represented, it was better than being a Livingston one second longer.

"Would you mind giving me and my wife a few moments alone?" Charlie pushed from the hood of his fancy sports car.

"I do mind," Miles said in a calm voice.

Too calm, and it rattled her fucking nerves.

"Too bad. I need to speak with Liberty alone and it doesn't concern you." Charlie inched closer, almost daring Miles to get in his face.

"Unless the lady asks me to leave, I'm not going anywhere. Besides, this is my shop. No one tells me what to do in my own place of business," Miles said. This time his tone shifted. It wasn't loud. Or cocky. But it did have an edge to it.

She wasn't sure if she was terrified or thrilled.

"Liberty, please ask this man to leave us alone." Charlie glared.

Just then, a police car rolled into the parking lot.

Rebecca Kirby eased from the driver's seat. Her long blond hair was pulled back into a bun and she was decked out in her uniform, badge, gun, and all.

Liberty had met her a dozen times in the café and Rebecca had always been kind. A little scary, but nice.

"Good afternoon." Rebecca looped her fingers through her belt. "I see we meet again." She nodded. "I hope I'm not going to be pulling you over for speeding or reckless driving in my town today."

"No, ma'am," Charlie said.

"Good to hear because that first time I was being kind. I could have suspended your license right then and there. Second time, I won't be so forgiving."

Charlie lifted his hands. "I've already apologized and it won't happen again."

"Hey, Ma," Miles said. "Thanks for coming."

"My pleasure. Now, what is this problem Liberty needs my help with?"

Miles handed her cell to his mother. "She needs you to make it very clear to this fine gentleman that she doesn't want him coming to her house or contacting her or Gabriel anymore. They're divorced and that's the end of it."

"You've got to be kidding me," Charlie mumbled. "What business of this is yours? Liberty, tell them they've got this all wrong."

"They don't." She folded her shaking arms across her chest. "I moved here to get away from you. I've asked you to leave me alone. I've especially asked you to let Gabriel get used to his new surroundings and you pull a stunt like coming to his place of work. And after I asked you not to stop by the house anymore. To stop calling and texting him." She sucked in a deep breath and let it out slowly. Her nerves were more than frazzled and it weren't for Miles and his mom, she would have surely caved. She had no back-bone when it came to Charlie. She'd tried. But he always managed to worm his way back into her life.

Not this time.

"Please, let us be. I don't want to have to keep saying it. You're confusing Gabriel. We both need a fresh start and you and I are never getting back together." There. She'd said it. In front of witnesses, one of which was a cop.

"I believe Miss Blue has made her position clear." Rebecca handed the phone to Liberty. "I hope I won't be getting a phone call that you're bothering her or her brother. I'd hate to make this a police matter and have to pull out my handcuffs." She lowered her chin. "I'd take that as your first and only warning." She turned her attention to Miles. "I'm heading over to Emmerson's place. Something about an impromptu pool party. All are welcome. I hope I'll see you and Liberty over there soon."

"You probably will." Miles leaned in and kissed his mother's cheek. "Love you, Ma."

"You too, son." Rebecca turned and with some serious cop swagger, she strolled back to her vehicle, climbed in, and drove off.

Miles squeezed Liberty's hip. "Why don't you go grab my car keys. They're on my desk." He literally turned her and gave her a good shove.

She glanced over her shoulder and took one tentative step as Miles inched closer to Charlie.

"Come back here and you'll have more than my mother to deal with and it won't be pretty," Miles said.

"Are you threatening me?" Charlie asked.

Miles shook his head. "Just telling you the facts. Now get off my property."

Charlie muttered something under his breath, but Liberty couldn't quite make it out. Whatever it was, she suspected it wasn't good.

She stood by the office door and watched Charlie slowly drive away.

Fuck. What had she done? If she believed for one second that Charlie would go away quietly, she was a dumbass.

$\mathcal{M}$iles' mood had gone from bad to worse. While the afternoon at his brother's house had gone well, and Gabriel had fun, seemingly unaware of the day's events, he still acted off.

Even for him.

He had checked his phone a half dozen times and with each glance, he became agitated. After dinner, it had gotten so bad, Liberty decided it was time to go home.

This time, Miles couldn't fault her for that.

Gabriel had one major outburst that had scared some of the children. Poor Gabriel had tried his own brand of self-soothing and removed himself from the situation, but the damage had been done and now the man felt like shit.

But kudos to Miles' family for not making a big deal out of it.

And better yet, Liberty hadn't treated Gabriel like a child.

Miles sat on Liberty's front porch, nursing a short glass of bourbon. The front door rattled and she joined him with the bottle and a glass for herself.

"How's Gabriel?" he asked.

"Playing a video game, but he wouldn't give me his phone." She tipped her head back and took a shot, before pouring another.

"Is his cell password protected?"

"Yep." She leaned back, stretching out her legs.

"Maybe it's time to get two new phones with new numbers. That way Charlie doesn't have either," he said.

"I'm inclined to agree with you, but remember, change doesn't come easy for Gabriel. I can't just yank his phone away willy-nilly. I need a reason. And it has to be a good one; otherwise, it will cause him stress and he's already going backward."

"A new phone is coming out next week. Tell him that you got a good deal and wanted the upgrade, but in order to do it, you had to get new numbers. And remind him how you've asked Charlie not to come around anymore."

"You've got an answer for everything, don't you?" She sighed. "My life isn't that simple."

"But it doesn't have to be that complicated. You make it that way."

"You think I treat him like a child and maybe I do when it comes to his emotions, but I've always respected his privacy." She held up a finger. "To a certain degree. I mean, I monitor who he talks to on the internet with those damn games, because he doesn't really understand the dangers fully. And when it comes to his phone, he doesn't have too many numbers in it."

"But he has Charlie's and that's who he's texting with, even though you've asked him not to. And we both know that's what upset him at Emmerson's."

"Gabriel's in part why I stayed with that prick for so long." She tugged her hair out of her ponytail and ran her fingers through the long blond strands. "Charlie wasn't always this manipulative when it came to Gabriel. Granted, he did use Gabriel to get to me, which looking back, I'm at a loss as to why. But sometimes I feel like you've been doing that."

"I honestly resent that statement." Miles cocked his head. "I've done no such thing."

"Really? You spent an entire month getting to know Gabriel before asking me out or even trying to get in my pants." She shook her head and let out a cold, dry laugh. "I hate it when people do that."

"Don't be crude about what happened between us. And I'm not Charlie," Miles said softly. "I don't have any clue what he did to you or why your marriage ended so badly. My mind fills with all sorts of crazy ideas. But trust me, my feelings for Gabriel have nothing to do with my attraction or how I feel about you. They are two completely separate things. And if you want to get into why I kept you at arm's length when we first met, I'm happy to tell you." He tapped his finger on her knee. "But if I do that, you have to tell me what happened with Charlie."

"Another manipulator," she muttered.

"Not really. More like negotiation and if you said no, I'd still tell you why I was distant at first. But I want to know about Charlie because I can help get him out of your life. Or have you forgotten what my side gig is?" He arched a brow. "But in order to do that, I need information."

"Right. The private investigator business. You're a jack of all fucking trades."

"You sure do like to swear," he whispered.

"When I lived in high society, it was frowned upon. But now that I don't have to act like some prim and proper lady, that I'm not, I can be myself and dropping the F-bomb now and again, well, it feels fucking good."

"That wasn't a judgment, just an observation." He tipped back his drink, letting the smoky flavor fill his mouth before swallowing. Normally, this time of night was his favorite. He'd kick back with a nice glass of bourbon and stare at the stars and the moon. It always calmed his mind and fed his soul. But not tonight. There were so many other things on his mind, one of which was making sure she understood that what happened between them he didn't take lightly. "You've been in town for two months and you work at the café where most of our community likes to hang out, including almost every woman I've ever dated. I've seen you serve a few of them and I'm sure you've gotten an earful from one or two."

She smiled. Then laughed. Loudly. "Yeah. Someone did mention you were a bit of a horn dog and that I should stay away."

"I'm not surprised my reputation preceded me." He needed to tread lightly in this conversation if he was going to prove his point.

"Lucy Ann did mention that it wasn't as bad as Trixi, or whatever her name was, made it out to be. Although, I will say that Trixi actually had a few nice things to say about you, which was shocking."

He smacked his hand against his forehead. "I had no idea you ran into her. Of all the women who could be spreading tales about me, it had to be that one." Miles swallowed. Trixi had been hurt and not just by Miles, but her family had done a number on her as well.

She'd been told to choose between them and Miles, only, at first, she hadn't informed Miles of that ultimatum. When he found out, that put him between a rock and a hard place. He'd never choose a woman over his family. Of course, unless the girl he was dating was a hardened criminal, his family would never ask him to do such an insane thing. There had been a part of Miles that had been touched by Trixi's dedication to him, except in the end, neither one could live with the consequences.

"What did you do to her?"

"I guess you could say I broke her heart." There was no sugarcoating this one. "We hooked up a couple of years ago."

"Hooked up? That's kind of a disgusting way of putting it."

"Perhaps that's the wrong word. She was the closest thing I've ever had to a relationship. But she knew who I was and my aversion to getting married. She thought she could tame this bad boy."

"Is that what you are? A womanizer?"

"I take offense to that word and that's not what happened," he said behind a clenched jaw. Just because he didn't want to settle down, get married, and pump out a bunch of babies, didn't mean he was a dick.

"According to her, you're incapable of being in a committed relationship with anything that doesn't require an oil change."

"That's her father speaking. Not her." Miles stared at the night sky. He couldn't be angry at Trixi for saying those words. By the time they'd broken up, Miles had successfully done exactly what her father had said he would. "Trixi and I were doomed from the start, even if I didn't have a reputation. She comes from a rich family with certain standards and I didn't fit the mold. If she was going to be with me, she had to give up her family and her money. I didn't think that was fair. Because I did care about her, I started pushing her away."

"That's what I'd call a coward."

"You can call me anything you want. Judge me however you see fit. But the real truth of the matter was that I didn't love Trixi like a man should love a partner. I hated her father for how he treated her and forced her into making a choice between me and the rest of her family, but it shouldn't have come down to that. Yet at the end of the day, I also wasn't going to be able to give her the two things she wanted most. A ring and a kid."

"You don't want a family?" Liberty asked.

"I didn't then. I honestly don't know what I want now." His answer shocked his system. Being a father had never been something he gave a second thought. A husband was out of the question. "I've struggled with a lot of things my entire life, one of which was watching my parents have a shitty-ass marriage. My mom had an affair when I was one and it produced my little brother."

"What?" Liberty's voice screeched.

"The worst part about that was my dad agreed to raise Jameson as his own until Steve, my mom's current husband, strolled back into town a few years ago, blowing my family into pieces. Add Jameson's divorce, a few brothers who had their hearts broken, and I chose to be a bachelor, because in my book, love sucks."

She raised her glass and tapped it against his. "Finally, something we both can agree on."

"You loved Charlie," he said as a statement of fact. "Why don't we shift gears and talk about that for a bit."

She set her glass on the steps and shifted, facing him dead-on. "One of the reasons I'm so guarded with you is because Charlie was a lot like you in the beginning. He adored Gabriel. He was so good with him and it warmed my heart to see someone treat my brother with kindness and respect, not pity. And Charlie showered me with gifts. I was reluctant at first. After my parents left me and Gabriel to fend for ourselves, I mistrusted everyone I ever knew in their circles, and that included Charlie. And especially his parents. They never accepted me. What's really weird is they begged me not to divorce their son." She shook her head and chuckled. "Their exact words were, *No Livingston gets divorced. Make this right.* They even tried to give me money and things in order to stay. They told me they would do anything if I stayed with Charlie. They even told me how broken Charlie was because I'd left him."

"Something tells me Charlie's never been broken-hearted over anything," Miles mumbled. "I find it interesting that it was his parents who were the ones that pleaded with you to remain in Palm Beach and in a marriage that made you miserable."

"Charlie can be a lot like Gabriel sometimes when he either feels hurt or doesn't get his way."

"What does that mean, exactly?" Miles asked.

"He'll tell me to fuck off. Dare me to leave. He's even let me walk out the front door, locking it behind me, always yelling from the other side that I'd be back. And he was right, I always did, because of Gabriel. It was too much to leave in the heat of the moment. I had to plan. That took time."

"That was smart on your part," Miles said. "I'm curious. What did his parents do to try to get you to stay?"

"A brand-new car showed up one day. There was all of a sudden talk of them paying for college. They bought Gabriel a new computer. Told him no more adult programs. They told me they'd change my prenup agreement, but no amount of money was going to make me stay. I mean, I did that twice before, and nothing changed. They never followed through anyway. It was all talk so I wouldn't drive right out of town. But I don't understand why. They don't even like me."

"How long were you married?" The wheels in Miles' backward brain began spinning wildly out of control. It was hard to contain it when he got going.

Thinking was never a problem. Sorting information was easy. Speaking not hard at all.

But he couldn't put it on paper if he tried.

He'd need Rhett for that one.

That was one of the reasons he'd never go to work full-time for his brother, and while everyone in his family totally believed he had the chops to be a PI or a cop, it was the test and the paperwork that made Miles twitch. His learning disability would never go away. It was something he'd accepted a long time ago and had overcome in many ways. But it didn't change the fact he still had it.

"I got married at twenty-one. I left him for good fourteen months ago, but the divorce didn't become final until two months ago, so a little over ten years."

"When did you try to leave before this final time?"

"Five years into the marriage." She flattened her hand against her stomach. "And then again three years after that."

He inhaled sharply. He'd watched too many of his sisters-in-law tell his brothers they were pregnant by merely covering their bellies. He knew what that gesture meant.

Only, he didn't know what happened.

"I know it's none of my business, but I'm going to ask anyway. Why did you try to leave? And why did you end up staying?"

"The first time I caught him cheating. I was more

upset that Gabriel was in the house than the fact he was fucking some bimbo."

"That's not cool."

"It would have crushed Gabriel and he wouldn't have understood." She let out a slow breath. "It's one of the reasons why I need to ease Gabriel into the idea of me dating anyone. Even someone he likes as much as you. I can't just throw you in his face."

"The man knows what sex is. He's asked me about it a few times, but yeah, the cheating part would have been confusing as hell since he does have some displaced loyalty with Charlie."

"He's a twenty-two-year-old virgin. There have been times I thought about hiring someone to have sex with him, but then I think about all the things that could go wrong." She laughed, lifting her drink. "The man is obsessed with porn and I can't bring myself to tell him to stop looking at it."

"A little self-gratification never hurt anyone."

"Sounds like you're speaking from experience."

He chuckled. "For the last four months, until last night, it's all I knew, but we're getting sidetracked." He reached out and tucked her hair behind her ear. "Something you're good at."

She shrugged.

"Why did you stay after he cheated on you?" he asked.

"We had been fighting for a year over whether or not to have a baby. I wanted to go back to school, and he wanted me to be the good little wife and stay at home. I was bored stiff and getting antsy. I refused to go off birth control and that was his way of paying me back."

"That's cruel."

She nodded. "But he said all the right things. Did all the right things. And we were good for a while, until I got pregnant." She rubbed her thumb over her index fingernail, picking at the edges. "It was as if I fulfilled my wifely duty and he went back to being a prick. He would stay out late with his buddies. He started ignoring Gabriel. He told me no more college. That was it. I was going to be a mother and that was my role. I felt trapped and alone."

"I imagine you would."

She wiped a few tears that dripped down her cheek. "When I was seven months pregnant, I had enough. I wanted out. I didn't care if he and his parents cut me and Gabriel off. I figured I'd be able to handle Gabriel because he was so excited about the baby. I also assumed that Charlie and everyone else would still be in our lives because of the baby, but I just couldn't live there anymore. It was pure torture. I was alone. No one cared. I was Rapunzel trapped in a tower without my long hair. I packed my bags and told him I was leaving. He dealt with it by shoving me down the stairs."

"He did what!" Miles jumped to his feet with his

fists clenched tightly at his sides. He paced in front of the porch, itching to punch something.

Anything.

The one thing he couldn't tolerate was anyone putting their hands on a woman. But one carrying a child? Somehow, that made it even worse.

"Please tell me you called the cops," he said, doing his best to rein in his rage.

"I hit my head and was knocked unconscious, so no," she said softly. "Gabriel found me and bless his soul, he called 9-1-1."

"Where the fuck was that dick of an ex-husband?"

"Off fucking his next conquest."

Miles' heart dropped like a brick to his toes. "He left you there? Pregnant with his kid? Passed out at the bottom of a staircase?"

"I really didn't need the blow-by-blow recount." She sighed. "But yeah. When I came to at the hospital, our little girl had been taken by an emergency C-section. I got to hold her for a little bit before she passed. But Charlie, he never even saw her."

Miles swallowed. Hard. He had no words for that and what he wanted to say wouldn't be kind. At all.

And that's not what Liberty needed.

He eased back onto the steps and looped his arm around her shoulders. "What does Gabriel know about this?"

"He thinks I fell down the stairs and he went

along with what Charlie and his parents said. That it was my fault that I lost the baby."

Miles pulled her tight, kissing her temple. "That wasn't your fault. What Charlie did was criminal and he should be rotting in a prison cell for what he did to you and your little girl."

"Maybe so, but I wasn't in the right frame of mind to deal with that. Gabriel was angry with me. You see, there was a step ladder at the top of the stairs because that was where there was a small library and he believed that I was on that, getting a book from a top shelf. I was so distraught and depressed, it took a while before I was able to pull myself out of it and get to a point where I could leave, but Gabriel will always believe that I was reckless."

"Not if you tell him the truth."

She leaned her body against Miles, dropping her head on his shoulder. "I've spent my entire life trying to protect him from some of the pains of this world. Our parents abandoning him because of who he is. Charlie and what he did to me. To us. Telling him won't bring back my baby. It won't change what happened. All it will serve is to make Gabriel angry at me for lying. Or confuse him about trust. I'm sure you think I'm wrong. And maybe I am. But if we're being completely honest here, I've never told a single soul about what really happened that day until right now."

"I'm glad you felt safe trusting me with it." He closed his eyes for a moment, doing his best to let go of the anger flowing through his veins, because if he ever saw that man again, his mother would be slapping the handcuffs on him, not Charlie. "I'll go buy two new phones tomorrow. I'll take Gabriel with me. It will be a surprise. I'll tell him it's a perk of working for me."

"I can't let you do that." She lifted her head. "Truth be told, I can't afford them right now."

"I'll put them on my plan and you can pay me back when you can." One thing Miles had learned from some of his sisters-in-law, especially Rumor and Bryn, was how important it was to feel that freedom of being on your own. "We can devise a payment plan of some kind. But I'm insisting. Charlie is more dangerous than I suspected and I'm not going to sit here and let him come after you, especially when I know he's fucking with Gabriel. Whether you want to believe it or not, I care about both of you."

She burst out laughing.

"I don't see why that's so funny."

"Trixi," she whispered. "Darlene. Andrea. Bonnie. Shall I go on?"

He groaned. "Look. I'm not a saint. And I'm certainly not asking you to move in with me or marry me. But I do like you and I want to see where this can go. Is there something wrong with that?"

"No. But considering what I was married to, you have to understand why I'm leery of dating… you."

"I don't cheat. I never have and I never will. Ask

any of them and they will tell you that." He cupped her face, drawing her closer until her lips were so close he could feel her hot breath on his skin. "I haven't been able to stop thinking about you since we met. I haven't looked at another woman since. I have no idea what that means. I only know that no other woman has turned my insides to mush the way you have." He kissed her, hard. It was wet, wild, and it had more passion behind it than he'd been prepared for.

But Liberty had successfully not only stolen his heart.

She'd sucked his soul right out of his body.

He couldn't see straight and when he did, all he saw was her and if he didn't explore what it meant, he'd always wonder if he'd either been sitting around waiting for the right woman to tame his crazy ways.

Or if he'd simply been a fool afraid to love.

She fisted his shirt, breaking off the kiss. She blinked. "I can't do this right now. Gabriel is in the family room," she whispered. "And you scare the crap out of me."

He jerked his head. "Why?"

"Because I can't afford to like anyone and I like you way too much. We keep doing this, and one of us will be doing the walk of shame again." She jumped to her feet. "Good night, Miles." She disappeared into the house.

She liked him. He smiled.

Now all he had to do was get rid of Charlie.

And by that, he meant, putting that asshole where he belonged.

In prison.

## 7

*L*iberty took the drink Trinity, Emmett's wife, handed her and leaned back in the recliner. The sun had dipped behind the horizon, and the moon and stars had begun to speckle the night sky. "You have a beautiful home. And this view? Holy crow. Watching the boats go up and down the Intracoastal has to be one of your favorite pastimes. Especially at night."

"Thank you." Trinity set her glass of wine on the table and plopped into her chair. She pointed to the baby monitor. "It's one of Leslie's favorite things to do, next to being out there with her daddy."

"I'm sorry she was so upset when the boys pulled away on the boat."

"She's six months old. She won't remember tomorrow. Besides, if I don't get her to bed between eight and nine, she'll be up till midnight and that's never fun for the adults. This way, she sleeps till five and she loves to have breakfast with her dad. Those two have such a sweet relationship that sometimes I feel guilty. All I have to do is deal with her while he's at work and that means sitting with her by the window while she waits for his car to pull in."

"That's too cute."

"It really is." Trinity smiled. "She lights up like a little baby Christmas tree every time Emmett walks in the room. There are times I get jealous because she doesn't have that visceral reaction to me, but when it's time to go to sleep, all she wants is her mama, so there's that."

"Babies certainly can be fickle." Liberty did her best to keep the memories at bay. It had only been a few precious moments that she had with her darling daughter. A few weak cries while the nurses did their best to comfort Liberty. Perhaps it was time to change the subject before she burst out in tears. "How long do you think the boys will be gone fishing?" Liberty had almost said no to hanging with Trinity when Miles first proposed it. But Gabriel had been too excited about the fishing excursion and there was no way she was going to burst his bubble.

Trinity glanced at her watch. "I'm sure they will be back within the hour. Emmett has to be at the station early."

"It's got to be hard to be married to a cop." Liberty sipped her wine. It was a nice dry red, which went with the cooler summer night. She crossed her legs at the ankles. It had been three days she'd seen or heard from Charlie. Not a single text or call.

However, she had changed her phone number, as well as Gabriel's, making it clear he wasn't to give them out.

That hadn't gone over too well at first. He didn't mind the new cell. That was shiny and pretty. But being told what to do regarding Charlie, well, Gabriel didn't like that. He had stormed off into his room and slammed the door. She had no idea if he contacted Charlie or not, but the good news was she hadn't heard from the man.

And even though he rented a place not far from Miles' mother and had an office outside of town, she hadn't crossed paths with him, and Gabriel hadn't either.

But as long as Charlie continued to live and work in Lighthouse Cove, it was only a matter of time.

Restraining order or not, Charlie didn't like to lose. He'd fought her on the divorce. He hadn't wanted to sign the papers. He'd done everything to try to stop it, including offering to go to counseling, but that was a little too late. He should have done that the first time she caught him cheating.

Or when she lost the baby.

Instead, he blamed her and told her to go and get her shit together. Their marital problems were her fault, not his, and it was her job to fix them.

Asshole.

"I bet you worry about him every time he leaves the house in uniform," Liberty said, pushing the thoughts of Charlie and her past out of her mind.

"I worry, but his job here is generally quiet." Trinity lifted the wineglass and took a dainty sip. She was a class act and while some of her mannerisms reminded her of the ladies at the country club, she was no snob, that was for damn sure. "In all the time I've known him, outside of what happened with my biological father and the night Rumor got shot, which was the same night Leslie was born, not much happens here. His job is mostly acting like a tough guy." Trinity leaned forward. "But it's his mother who's the badass. She still scares the crap of me, let me tell you. And she's seventy."

"Holy shit. I didn't realize she was that old. She certainly doesn't look it. I saw her in action when she dealt with my ex-husband. Somehow, I think the universe was kind when she had all boys and not a daughter in sight."

"That's a true statement." Trinity laughed. "Nathan really wants her to retire. He wants her job in the worst way and he deserves it. I actually think she's going to do it this year. She's working less and less and she loves hanging out with all her grandkids. She's so much softer with them than she was with the boys. At least that's what they all tell me."

"That's a grandparent's prerogative." Not that

Liberty knew anything about that. When Sadie had been born, Charlie's parents didn't bother to come visit for two days. Their pathetic excuse had been they thought she needed time alone.

Bullshit.

Charlene and Oswald were too busy with whatever parties they were attending to give her a second thought.

"If she's going to actually give up the badge, it will be next month." Trinity lifted her glass. "Let's hope she does it. All the boys love their mother and have enjoyed working for her, but it's time for Nathan to take over. He'll do it for ten years, then maybe Emmett will for two or three. After that." Trinity shrugged. "Well, this town might see a chief of police who doesn't have the last name Kirby for the first time in like forever."

"What about Emmerson? Doesn't he want to be chief?"

Trinity laughed. "God, no. He loves being a cop, hates managing people, and there's a good chance he retires when his baby is born. He's been talking about getting his PI license and working with Rhett while helping Jameson expand his handyman business."

"All the Kirby boys have so much in common, yet they are all so different." Not that she really knew any of them, but they were all staples at the diner. Everyone in town knew who they were and for the most part, they all had good things to say about each and every one.

Except Miles.

But that was just a handful of women who had either heard she was living next door or who had seen her chatting with him and made it their life's work to warn her off because he'd done them wrong somehow. But even they didn't say he was a bad person, just not dating material, unless all you wanted was a good time because that's all Miles was capable of.

"All you really need to know about them is they are good people and they will show up when you need them, and sometimes when you don't." Trinity laughed. "So, tell me. What's going on with you and Miles?"

"Absolutely nothing." She took a big gulp of her wine. Only that man had gotten under her skin and tickled all her girly parts. The ones she thought her ex-husband had successfully killed. Miles ignited a fire in her belly and it had roared to life and no matter how many times she tried to put it out, a spark caught and it exploded.

He crept into her daily thoughts and visited her dreams.

She'd never sworn off men. But she had tabled the idea of them until she got on her own two feet. She needed to know she could take care of herself, and her brother, before she allowed anyone back in her life. It wasn't that she didn't want a life partner, she did. But she had a lot of shit to deal with before that happened.

"You're kidding, right?" Trinity swung her legs over the side of her chair. "Isn't this a double date?"

"With a fifth wheel named Gabriel?" Liberty did her best to make a joke, but it fell flat. "No. It's not. I just couldn't say no to Gabriel and honestly, when Miles said you'd be here and I'd have girl time, I jumped at it."

"That's a nice compliment and I'm certainly having fun getting to know you better." She set her glass down and adjusted her hair. "But I have to ask. Are you not interested in Miles because of his reputation as a ladies' man or are you just not into him?"

Now that was a loaded question. One she wasn't quite sure how to answer. Maybe being honest might help her sort it out. "Can I be honest? Without it being repeated?"

Trinity raised her hands. "This is the circle trust. I'm not telling anyone, including my husband."

"Do you have any idea how many women have warned me off at the café? It's laughable. Has he really left that many broken hearts behind?"

"No." Trinity sighed. "But some of those girls have taken him on as a challenge. Especially in the last couple of years. It's like they have all gotten together and made a little pact about who can tie that man down. I'm not even sure any of them liked him that much going in. It was all about who could get him to fall in love. Wrong way to go about things if you ask me, and Miles, he's got some dumb ideas about love and what it means. Watching all his brothers fall hard, it's softened him to the concept, but he thinks it will change him and he has some other issues."

"But you have to agree as a woman madly in love with her husband that it does change you."

"I suppose it does, but not for the worse. Only, that's what he grew up with and he's guarded himself." Trinity leaned a little closer. "I don't know if you know anything about his childhood. But that poor man was picked on relentlessly as a kid."

"I heard a little about that and his learning disabilities."

"It was horrible for him and he still struggles. He also has generalized social anxiety," Trinity said. "Last year, there was a massive party in honor of his mom. He really didn't want to go, but we all talked him into it. He was a mess. Even with all the coping skills he's learned over the years, he ducked out early. Crowds are not his thing."

"Mine either, but for different reasons," she said softly. "I understand why he's so good with Gabriel."

"Miles understands misfits because he thinks he's one and while he'll never say this out loud, he doesn't believe he's good enough for any woman. It's why he has these stupid short-lived flings, except for Trixi, though I wasn't around for that."

"He told me about her, but only after I got an earful from her and asked him about it."

Trinity blinked. "He's almost never honest about that one. He doesn't like to admit how much he actually cared about her. He once got real with his brothers and told them he was afraid a girl would stick around long enough and find out he was just a dumb man incapable of taking care of her properly, which is something Trixi's father drilled into his head. The next morning he chalked it up to being drunk."

Liberty opened her mouth, but only a gasp escaped. She cleared her throat. "That's kind of sad."

"It is." Trinity rested her hand on Liberty's knee. "I see the way both of you look at each other. It's not lost on any of us. But Miles is the kind of man who gives up when a girl shows little to no interest and we all know he's asked you out and you've said no at least four times. He hasn't called it quits."

"He's helping me with my ex-husband and my little brother does work for him, so there's that." Liberty stared into her drink. Her cheeks flushed.

"Holy shit. Something has happened between the two of you." Trinity held up her hand. "I think I need to repeat my question about what's preventing you from continuing to date my brother-in-law."

"That's not necessary," Liberty said, realizing she wasn't getting out of this conversation, and it did feel good to talk to another female she could trust. "His reputation is troubling. Not only for me, but because of Gabriel. I'm also not sure I'm ready to even think about dating."

"But you slept with him."

Liberty tried not to smile, but it was impossible.

"And you liked it." Trinity gave Liberty's leg a little shove.

"He is incredibly sexy. Charming. Kind. And everything a woman could want in a man. Which makes me believe he's just too damn good to be true and all those women are right. On the other hand, a fling wouldn't be the worst thing in the world, if only I knew I could protect Gabriel and it wouldn't affect his relationship with Miles."

"I can understand your concern there, but trust me when I say, Miles isn't that guy," Trinity said with conviction. "All those women, they don't know the real Miles because he doesn't let them in. He barely ever brought any of them around the family. When we have family gatherings, he comes alone." Trinity waggled her brows. "He would have never brought someone over here when he wanted to go fishing with Emmett. Or invite a girl to his brother's wedding. He doesn't mix his love life with his family. He wouldn't want any of those ladies to think what they had with him stood a chance. And he wouldn't want to give us the wrong impression."

"And what impression is he giving you now?" Liberty asked with her heart hammering in the center of her chest.

"Um, that man has it bad and he wants something different out of life."

The sound of boat engines and men laughing filled the air. Liberty sat up taller as Emmett pulled the fishing boat toward the lift.

"One last thing before we're bombarded by testosterone," Trinity said. "I know you've got a lot going on in your life right now. And on the outside, Miles doesn't look like the kind of guy you'd want to get involved with, but trust that he's one of the best men you could ever have on your side. He'd never do anything to intentionally hurt you or Gabriel. He's honest. He'll never lie to you. He might get cold feet and start pushing you away, but if he does that, you'll know it's because he's scared of how he feels and his insecurities are getting the better of him. All you need to do is call him on them."

"I don't know. I want to go for it because it would be different and something that I don't have to consider the future. I can live in the moment for a change," Liberty whispered. "But—"

"No buts. Do you like him?"

"That's not even the point."

"Look. Miles has closed himself off for two reasons. One of them I understand. Watching what his parents went through was rough. But all he needs is one good woman to show him he's good enough. All he needs to learn is that love isn't all bad."

"Oh, and you think I'm that woman?" Liberty glared. "I just told you I'm not looking for love."

Trinity shrugged. "I certainly wasn't looking for love when I walked into this town, but it came up and bit me in the ass. Go out with Miles. See what's there. What's the worst that can happen? Besides good sex, because by that smile and the twinkle in your eye, I'd say that man rocked your world."

Liberty laughed. "That's one way of putting it." Lighthouse Cove was her fresh start in life. It was her chance at a new beginning. A new chapter. There was no reason she had to live under a rock and Miles wasn't a bad man. He was kind. Considerate. Generous.

A date wouldn't kill her.

Actually, it might do her some good.

Besides, even if it went nowhere, the one thing she did see was that all these women who warned her off Miles were still friendly with the man. That had to mean something. That at the very worst, he wouldn't break Gabriel's heart.

---

Miles once again found himself sitting on Liberty's front porch with a short glass of bourbon. He should get up and leave. He wasn't even sure if Liberty was going to come back out and say goodbye. She'd made it clear they were done for the evening when she told him it was late and Gabriel needed to go to bed.

But she had given him a drink, so there was that and by damn, he was going to finish it.

Just one of the many mixed messages she'd been giving him all night. Damn, if he didn't suck at relationships. He could do flings. He could do a good time. But the last time he tried to have a real connection with a woman, he broke her heart.

He could live with himself if he did that to Liberty, only he couldn't let it go. It was as if she was the air that filled his lungs. The food that fueled his body. He'd never needed anyone, except his family.

And now he found himself needing her in ways he couldn't fathom.

He stared out into the dark night. A few neighbors strolled by and waved. He'd always enjoyed living in the heart of town, near the hustle and bustle of what little action Lighthouse Cove offered. He could walk to a few local watering holes for a drink or dinner, since cooking for one kind of sucked.

But lately, he had the itch to move to the water and closer to one of his brothers. It wasn't that he was all that far. It was only a three-mile walk to Emmerson's place and Jameson was only a few streets from that. But the pull to be near that liquid gold had called to his heart.

He never had a reason to want a big house with a pool on the Intracoastal. He had brothers who provided all those fun extras. And a mother who had a mansion. What more could he possibly want?

The sound of the front door screeched across the floorboards.

Liberty.

That's what he wanted and it had messed with his head, not to mention his heart. He couldn't make sense of his feelings and he was plumb tuckered out from trying.

He liked women. Always had and there was nothing wrong with that. He just didn't like having them in his space all the time. Or dealing with what came with real relationships. The commitment. The responsibility.

The hurt.

But mostly that he wasn't good enough.

Fuck. He needed to stop that train of thought.

"I'm just about finished." He raised his drink to his lips and sipped, savoring the last few drops.

"You don't have to rush off." She waved the bottle and eased into the chair next to him. "I'm sorry if I was a little harsh when we got home. But Gabriel was exhausted. He was on the verge of a meltdown and I didn't want him to think he was going to miss out on something. He can have the worst FOMO, especially when it comes to you and your family these days."

Miles chuckled. "He had so much fun reeling in those fish. He was like a kid in the candy store. I don't know what I enjoyed more. Watching him or spending time with you, my brother, and Trinity."

"He couldn't stop smiling." She set the bottle between them on the floor and sighed. "Thank you for taking him, but I have no idea how to cook those filets. I'm a killer cook when it comes to breakfast, but dinner, I'm limited to casseroles."

"Why don't I grill them up nice for us tomorrow night." What he should do was stop trying. Not only was Liberty one of the few women who was immune to his charm, even if they had shared one hell of an evening in his kitchen, but she was definitely way too good for him and even if he could get her to agree to date him, it wouldn't last.

This time it wouldn't be because he couldn't bring himself to be a one-woman man, but because she'd figure out he wasn't ever going to be anything other than a grease monkey.

A successful one, but he had his own set of issues and he knew his limitations. He'd accepted them and for the last forty-one years, he'd learned to embrace them.

Why go fucking with what worked.

And there was that damn tape again. No matter how hard he tried to stop it from blending into his thoughts, he couldn't.

"I wouldn't want to put you out. You do so much for us as it is." She swirled her glass before taking a gulp. "I want you to know how much I appreciate it."

He loved that she drank the same brand of bourbon he did.

"It's no trouble. There was a lot of meat on those fish. What doesn't get eaten can be used for fish tacos the next night."

"That's smart." Liberty nodded. "I had a lot of fun with Trinity. I really like her."

"She's a good person and she'll be a good friend."

"I hate to bring this up, but did Gabriel look at his phone at all while you were out on the boat?"

"Not once." Miles was happy to report that fact. "Have you heard from or seen your ex-husband?"

"I haven't and I don't know if that's good or bad."

"Emmett said no one has seen him since he showed up at my shop three days ago. Maybe my mother scared him off."

"That would be nice, but Charlie doesn't frighten that easily. Knowing him, he's regrouping."

Miles leaned over, lifted the bottle, and poured one finger. Just one more small glass and then he'd call it a night. She knew how he felt and what he wanted. The ball was in her court. "You know what to do if he shows up."

"I do, but I don't like it." She adjusted her baseball cap, pulling it down, making it so he couldn't see her beautiful blue eyes sparkling in the moonlight.

There wasn't a single thing he didn't like about Liberty. She was easy to talk to or just sit and be with. Even though she had a lot on her mind, she could be laid-back. Her life had been riddled with pain, but she didn't wallow in self-pity. She picked herself up by her bootstraps and kept on pushing forward. And she certainly didn't hold any punches.

"I worry about how Gabriel will respond," she said. "While he's handling the separation from Charlie well right now, who knows what will happen when that man shows his ugly face."

"Gabriel's never alone. He's always either with you or me. He'll have all the support he needs."

"I don't know how to thank you. This goes way beyond being neighborly. Or being his boss."

Miles sighed. It sure did and he didn't know how to explain it to her, much less himself. He was torn between asking her out again and getting up, walking home, and going to bed alone. Not once in his adult life had he ever found himself in this situation. All the women he dated were never meant to be serious, except Trixi. The ones who had other plans, he dropped like a hot potato, but even they didn't want him for the long haul.

They wanted the challenge.

And he was glad to play for a short time.

Even though once or twice that had been a whopper of a mistake, like with Trixi. That one he had regretted. She was a nice girl and deserved better than his sorry ass.

But so did Liberty, which left him between a rock and a hard place.

"Wow. You're deep in thought." She nudged his arm. "I don't think I've ever seen you this quiet or melancholy. What's gotten into you?"

How the fuck did he answer that one? He tipped his head back and downed the last drop of his bourbon. It soured his belly. He set the tumbler down and stood. "I should go. It's late."

She jumped to her feet and curled her precious fingers around his biceps. "Have I done something to upset you?"

"No. Not at all." He lifted the cap off her head, turning it and placing it backward so he could see her pretty eyes better.

Mistake.

Those blue pools fucking captivated him and drew him in like a spotlight in the harbor guiding the ships home at night.

"Then why are you running off and acting like someone sucker punched you in the gut?"

"You want me to answer that honestly?"

"Yes." She nodded.

He blew out a puff of air. He was fully clothed, and yet he felt totally naked. "I can be your neighbor. Your friend. Your confidant. I have no problem doing that. But I need a moment to switch into that gear, and sitting out here with you any longer, I'll want to do something stupid like take you to bed again. I can handle rejection. Happens all the time. But for whatever reason, when you do it, it does feel like I got kicked in the stomach and I'd rather walk away before I make an ass out of myself or you have to toss me off this porch."

She rested her hands on his shoulders. "I'm not going to ask you to leave." She leaned into him, tilting her head.

Gripping her hips, he held his breath while his heart beat wildly in the center of his throat. He swallowed.

"I know who you are, Miles. And you certainly know enough about the baggage I bring to the table." She pressed her lips against his mouth in an exotic dance. "This is me agreeing to go out on a date with you, and more."

He arched a brow. "Seriously?"

"Do I have to repeat myself?"

"God, no." He wrapped his arms around her and kissed her, hard. It was the kind of kiss that let a woman know she was desired. Wanted. That she was the only woman he was thinking of and that there would be more to come. He palmed her cheek. "This is going to sound strange, but what about Gabriel?"

"He can take care of himself for a few hours."

"I'm not leaving him alone while your asshole of an ex is unaccounted for. I don't trust Charlie as far as I can throw him. Maybe Gabriel can hang with one of my brothers for an evening."

"I'm sure he'd like that."

"All right then, but not tomorrow night. We're

going to cook that fish. Gabriel deserves to eat what he caught."

She smiled. "You're a good man, Miles."

"Don't tell anyone." He kissed her cheek. "I'll see you tomorrow." He jogged down the stairs, pausing at the bottom to glance over his shoulder and wave.

And just like that, he had a date.

With Liberty.

"Hey, wait," Liberty called.

He paused, glancing over his shoulder. "What?"

"You must have missed the part where I mentioned more." She smiled.

"No. I heard that." He chuckled. "But let's save it for our date. I want to do it right this time. Not have you stealing my shirt and scurrying across the yard afterward."

"Have it your way." She blew him a kiss.

Fuck. He was in way over his head and he knew it.

This called for a little advice from one of his brothers. But which one?

He'd decide that tomorrow. For now, he'd go climb into bed and dream about the sweet girl who lived next door.

Liberty handed Gabriel a tall soda and sat on the park bench. "How are things going at the shop?"

"I love my job." Gabriel slurped on his soda before reaching for the bag of food. "Miles is so smart. He knows everything about cars. And I mean everything. Motorcycles too. It's hard to believe he has that processing thing because there isn't anything he doesn't know when it comes to a motor or rebuilding any vehicle."

"He's certainly learned to compensate for it. Much like you." Liberty pulled out her sandwich and opened the wrapper.

"Are we going to stay in Lighthouse Cove?" Gabriel fiddled with his French fry packet.

"We own that house. This is the place I wanted to make our home. Don't you like it here?"

Gabriel continued to stare at his food. Difficult conversations made it harder for him to make eye contact, even with his big sister, the only constant in his life. "I do really love it here. But sometimes it feels like there's a storm brewing."

That was a big analogy for Gabriel to make and she wasn't sure if it was because Charlie wasn't coming around and Gabriel was smart enough to know that when he did, it could be bad. Or if it was something else entirely. "What do you mean?"

Gabriel shrugged. "You say things are over with you and Charlie, but are they really?"

She let out a long breath. "I'm so sorry that my divorcing Charlie has hurt you, but yes. He and I are over and we will never get back together." She took her brother's hand. "I can't have him coming around."

Miles and everyone in his family believed that a little truth wouldn't hurt Gabriel. If anything, it might keep him safe. And Miles was right. She did tend to treat her brother like a baby.

"Charlie has done some things that I can't forgive him for," she said softly.

"Like what?" Slowly, Gabriel lifted his gaze, but it wasn't to catch hers. Instead, he stared off toward the inlet.

"I don't know if this is the right time to get into the specifics and it's not fair for me to pull you into mine and Charlie's problems. Besides, they're done.

It's over. All you need to know is that in the end, he was not a good husband to me and he's not respecting my wishes. I want to start over here and I need him to let us do that. Him moving here and coming around is interfering with me starting a new life."

"Is that why you filed some order that can have Charlie arrested if does come near you?" Gabriel asked, clenching his fists on his lap.

"How did you know about that?" she asked in a calm voice, even though her insides were raging.

Fucking Charlie.

"And please be honest with me, Gabriel. We're all each other has. I'm doing my best here not to coddle you or treat you like you're a kid. But I also don't want to upset you to the point you go off the deep end."

"Charlie called me and told me before we got the new phones and you told me not to give him the new number," Gabriel said. His tone was void of any real emotion, but his body language said something entirely different.

When he was angry, he usually stood, paced, and often tugged at his hair.

But he didn't do that.

Instead, he rocked slowly, back and forth, with his fists rubbing his thighs.

Fear.

But of what?

"Charlie shouldn't have told you that," she said. "I should have and I'm sorry I didn't sooner."

"I don't understand. What did he do that was so bad? I mean… I know… I saw some things and I… I… I… know you cried a lot. But Charlie says he loves you."

"He doesn't love me." Liberty took Gabriel's hand. "That is not what real love looks like. I get this is confusing and it's not what I brought you here to talk about, but I'm glad we did."

"I want to know what Charlie did," Gabriel said. "Please tell me."

She nodded. "But not right now. Not here. Let's do it tonight after dinner."

"Okay."

"I'd like to switch gears and chat about something else."

"Is this going to be heavy too?" He folded his arms. "This is why I feel like there's a big storm coming."

"It's not some big thing, but it is something I wanted to discuss with you before it happened."

Gabriel sighed. "What is it?" he said curtly, lowering his gaze.

She might as well go for broke. "Miles asked me to go on a date with him."

"Did you turn him down again?" Gabriel dunked a fry into the ketchup.

"No. This time I accepted."

He dropped the fry in his lap.

Liberty wanted to laugh, but she refrained. Instead, she handed Gabriel a napkin, opting not to treat him like a child and clean it up for him.

"Why? When?" Gabriel lifted his head.

"Because I kind of like him." She found herself smiling. "And he wants to take me to dinner tomorrow night. His brothers Rhett and Jameson have offered to take you fishing while this date happens."

Gabriel narrowed his stare. "I don't need babysitters."

"I know. That's not what this is. They're going anyway and thought you'd like to come." For obvious reasons, she left out the fact she didn't want him to be alone because of Charlie. "It's up to you," she added, hoping that would be all he needed to make the right choice.

"I like Miles' family. And like fishing. It's fun."

"Then it's settled. Rhett will pick you up at the shop when you're done working tomorrow and bring you home later and I'll go on a date with Miles." She bit into her burger.

"He likes you. A lot."

"And what makes you say that?"

"A man knows these things." Gabriel waved a fry in the air and smiled a cheeky grin as if he held all the answers. This was the Gabriel she loved. The one who went through life like he didn't have a care in the world. "Do you really like him?"

"I wouldn't have agreed to go out with him if I didn't."

"You went back to Charlie after you lost the baby and you didn't like him," Gabriel said. His words were laced with thick emotion. He'd been the only one to stay by her side when she lost her little girl.

She blinked. They hadn't talked about the baby she lost in a long time. It had not only been too painful for her, but Gabriel had blamed her for what happened. He'd been poisoned by Charlie's lies. Gabriel had cried for days over that loss and when he'd finally been able to put it behind him, they never spoke of it again. Of course, she was too scared to bring it up.

"Things were complicated," she said softly. "We all needed a little time to heal before we could leave." That was about as good of an answer as any.

"But you still didn't like him. Or love him." Gabriel continued to munch on his fries. "And I want to know why."

She wanted to tell him to eat his freaking burger, but she refrained. This conversation was hard enough. "You're right, I didn't love him," she admitted. "And I'm sorry I put you through all that, but now is not the time to get into this."

"After you lost the baby, Charlie asked me if you tried to lie to me about what happened. He told me if you did, I was to come to him."

Liberty froze. She couldn't breathe if she tried.

Her muscles burned. The roar of her blood racing through her body as her pulse pounded in her ears was the only thing she could hear. She swallowed the bile that smacked the back of her throat.

But it didn't go down.

The bitter taste lingered like three-day-old fish.

"The truth is both Charlie and I lied," she said behind gritted teeth while she did her best to keep the tears at bay. "Charlie made up a story about how I fell and I never corrected anyone, so the blame was placed on me."

"I don't even know what that means." Gabriel slammed his fists on the table. "Why do you talk in circles or in ways I can't understand? I can't make sense of your words. Charlie says it flat out. You climbed up on a ladder and—"

"Stop it," she said sternly. "Did you ever think for one second that this might be too painful for me? What happened has nothing to do with you and everything to do with why Charlie needs to be out of my life. He lied about what happened. He knows he did, but I was too distraught to do anything about it. I had just lost my little girl. I was scared and alone and it was all Charlie's fault."

"How was it his fault? He wasn't even there," Gabriel yelled.

She swiped at her eyes. "But he was there, Gabriel," she whispered. "I don't want to talk about this." She swallowed a guttural sob. "It's just too painful for me. I can see all the mistakes I've made and I'm trying to correct them. But I don't want to hurt you. Please trust me when I say that Charlie isn't who you think he is and it's my fault that you believe he is. I'm only trying to protect you."

"By lying to me." Gabriel went back to eating his fries. "I haven't contacted Charlie. And I won't. At least not for now. But I deserve to hear your truth so I can make up my mind about all this for myself."

She blew out a puff of air. Her little brother just surprised the fuck out of her by his response.

Miles.

He meddled.

Fuck.

She wasn't sure how she felt about that and she needed to have a conversation with Miles because it wasn't his fucking place.

"Tonight. After dinner."

"Miles is coming over. And then he'll stay for some bourbon. He always does," Gabriel said.

"I'll ask him to leave, and then I'll answer all of your questions." She rested her hand on her brother's leg. "But this won't be easy for you to hear and I understand I kept it from you, not because I didn't believe you could handle the truth, but because it wasn't your business. It was between me and Charlie. But also because I didn't want to destroy the bond you had with Charlie with a speeding bullet. I wanted to do it slowly, so that we could move on naturally. Organically. Make a new life for ourselves."

"The only thing I know is that either you're lying to me or Charlie is." He finally lifted his burger and took a bite. "I've been listening to Charlie for years about all this. But never you. The only thing you told me was that you didn't love Charlie anymore and that's why you divorced him. I'm not stupid. I have eyes. I know there's more."

She sighed. "Tonight. The whole sordid story. Tonight."

Miles reached for the bourbon and two short glasses.

Liberty came up behind him and curled her fingers around his biceps. "Not tonight," she said. "I'm sorry, but I'm going to have to ask you to leave. I need to have a long chat with my brother."

"Is everything okay?" Miles asked.

"Not really." She took the bourbon from his hands and set it on the counter. She yanked him through the kitchen and out the back door. "What the hell did you say to Gabriel about me and Charlie?" She planted her hands on her hips and glared.

If looks could kill, he'd be flat on his back, bleeding out on the grass.

He raked his fingers through his hair, which was in desperate need of a good cut. "I'm not sure what you're talking about." But knew exactly what she was referring to, only he didn't expect it to come back and bite him in the ass so quickly.

"He grilled me at lunch today about me lying to him about why I left Charlie. He demanded I tell him my truth. The words he used were not his own. As if someone coached him on what to say to me." She cocked her head and pursed her lips.

If she wasn't so fucking mad, he'd think the look was sexy as hell.

"He grilled me too," Miles admitted. "It started with asking me if I'd ever been in love before and if I had, why did those relationships end. I had to tell him that I've never experienced love before but that I've watched one of my brothers get divorced, along with my parents, and a couple end engagements and why those happened. Unfortunately for me, I didn't get right away where he was going with it. Sometimes, I'm not the sharpest tool in the shed."

"I don't buy that for one second." She poked him in the chest. "You're one of the smartest, most insightful men I know."

"Ouch." He rubbed his pec and narrowed his stare. "It's the truth. I don't always see where people are going with things. It's a processing issue."

"Bullshit." She folded her arms. "Don't hide behind your learning disability for this one. Now I'm stuck having to be honest when I'm not ready. This isn't only about Gabriel. But about me. I don't want to relive this shit. I just want to move forward with my life."

"So does Gabriel, but he doesn't understand why he can't be friends with Charlie." He pressed his finger over Liberty's lips when she opened her mouth. "After I told him about my parents, he was struck with the concept that they were still friends. That we all still got together as a family. Or how Emmett was still friendly with Melinda, even though their engagement ended kind of badly. Even I'm friends with some of my exes. All he wants is to understand this restraining order. I'm sorry that I overstepped, but I honestly didn't realize that's where he was going."

"What you fail to grasp is what this does to me. There are things I don't want him to know. Things I don't want anyone to know. It's not worth going through the pain, but now you've left me no choice." She glanced over her shoulder before giving her attention back to him. "Don't meddle again. I don't care if you mean well or not. This is my life, not yours." She turned on her heel and marched back inside, closing the door.

*Click.*

Locked.

Damn.

He pulled out his cell.

**Miles:** *Do you have time to meet me at the café for a cup of coffee and a chat?*

**Emmerson:** *I'm picking up Rumor shortly, so sure. But I don't have much time.*

**Miles:** *Understand. See you soon.*

He tucked his phone into his back pocket and meandered between the houses and down the street toward the center of town. The café was only a few blocks away and even at a slow pace, he'd be there in fifteen minutes.

As he passed Lucky's Bar and Grill, he noticed Charlie's fancy sports car in the parking lot. He paused for a second, contemplating going in and giving that man a piece of his mind.

Or maybe a fist sandwich.

He double-timed it to the café. Getting into an altercation with Charlie wouldn't do anyone any favors. But he did quickly send a text to every member of his family that Charlie was back in town. He also texted Liberty, letting her know too.

No response.

Deep in conversation, probably.

God, he hoped that went well.

Miles strolled into the Safe Harbor Café and waved to his sister-in-law Rumor, who raced from behind the counter to greet him with her arms wide open.

The woman was a breath of fresh air and the best damn thing that had ever happened to Emmerson. She might have blown through town with drug dealers on her tail and a boatload of secrets. But she landed right where she needed to be and stole Emmerson's heart and soul. Miles loved sitting back and watching it happen. He knew the second he saw Emmerson with Rumor that his brother was going to marry that girl. So did everyone in his family, even if Emmerson fought it tooth and nail.

"Hey, good-looking." She hugged him and kissed his cheek. "What are you doing here? I thought you were having dinner over at Liberty's tonight." Her face paled a little as she placed her hand over her stomach.

"Just finished," he said. "But she and her brother have some things they need to discuss, without me hanging around."

"Uh-oh. You sound a little bitter about that."

"I'm not bitter," he said. "Just feeling a little sheepish since I might have meddled where I don't belong and now she's pissed."

"Want to talk about it?" She waved her hand toward the counter.

"I'm actually meeting your husband here in a few minutes." He pointed to the corner booth. "Mind if we sit over there?"

"It's all yours. Can I get you a drink to start?"

"Bourbon on the rocks." He curled his fingers around her forearm. "Are you okay? You look like a ghost."

"Just tired. Doc said first trimester could be like that." She smiled. "I'll bring that drink right out."

He slipped into the booth, setting his cell on the table, face up. Not only did he want to know if Liberty texted, but the rest of his family. Chris Manzo had been looped in and he was working the night shift, so he would be the one keeping an eye on Charlie.

The bell over the door dinged.

Emmerson entered, proudly wearing his Lighthouse Cove police uniform. He stood a little over six foot and was a broad man.

Rumor greeted Emmerson by resting her head on his chest. He wrapped his arms around his wife and held her close for a moment before kissing her temple. "Give me a few minutes with Miles, then I'll take you home."

"Hey, little brother." Emmerson slipped into the booth.

Rumor brought over a cup of coffee for Emmerson and short glass with two fingers of bourbon for Miles.

"What's up?" Emmerson lifted his coffee and blew before taking a small sip.

"I might as well jump right in." He held his brother's gaze. "You'd think I, of all people, would understand women, but I haven't a fucking clue."

Emmerson burst out laughing.

"It's not funny."

"I'm sorry, but it's fucking hilarious." Emmerson leaned back, lifting his arm over the bench, and grinned like there was no tomorrow. "You know how to charm a woman whom you want to sleep with. You're an expert at keeping them at arm's length when you're with them. You know how to be cash register honest in the sense that you never promise anyone a rose garden. You're even damn good at letting them down easy so somehow they remain friendly-ish. But you're right, you don't *believe* you know dick about being in a relationship with a woman."

"You really know how to make a man feel like shit." Miles lifted his drink and took a gulp. "Is that really how everyone sees me?"

"Yes and no." Emmerson folded his hands on the table and leaned forward. "You want to get real?"

"Sure," Miles mumbled.

"The key word in my statement was *believe.* Ever since you were little, you felt different."

"Jesus Christ. I don't need this fucking lecture."

"Actually, you do. Same way I needed everyone in this family to tell me to stop closing myself off when Rumor walked into my life." Emmerson tapped his finger on the table. "I'm not going to sit here and discount your learning disabilities. We all know those are real. And because of them, and perhaps the way Mom treated you, which sucked, that gave you a shit ton of anxiety. We all watched it and did what we could to help you. We supported you in your decisions and went to bat for you with Mom." He raised his hand. "But not because you're different. We did it because you needed to find your path. The one that would give you the successes and show you that you're a fucking really smart man. Unfortunately, there are people who have put down your profession, which has only added to your inability to feel comfortable in your own skin."

"I know I'm good at what I do. I'm just not good at some of the business side of it." Miles stared at the cubes in his drink. It pissed him off sometimes that he couldn't manage his own books. That he needed someone else to manage that part of his business. Rhett and Jameson had done it for years. And now Trinity was doing it. That had always remained in the family and he valued and appreciated it.

But it was a constant reminder of what he wasn't capable of doing for himself.

"We all have our strengths and weaknesses. Look at me. There is no fucking way I'd ever make for a good chief of police. Nathan has always been a good cop, but he's better in the station managing people and doing the political side of this business. Can you imagine me doing that?"

Miles laughed. "God, no. You'd suck at it."

"My point exactly. But let's circle this back to women." He arched a brow. "We can start with Trixi."

"What does she have to do with anything?"

"Come on, man. You really liked her. More than

any girl you ever dated. One could say you might have been falling in love with that girl. You can tell everyone else otherwise. That you let it go on too long and she got the wrong idea. But the real reason that ended was because her father didn't like you. More importantly, he didn't like what you did for a living. He called you a grease monkey. He constantly told Trixi that you weren't good enough for his little girl and you let that get to you, especially when you learned he planned on cutting her off if she stayed with you." Emmerson leaned forward. "And then you went and broke her heart."

Miles lifted his tumbler but ended up setting it on the table instead of taking a sip.

Emmerson was right.

He could lie to himself, or anyone else for that matter, but the truth had just slapped him across the face.

There had been a part of him that had wanted to see if he could go the distance with Trixi. He had strong feelings for her and the word *love* tickled his brain during the time he spent with her. He had never been sure if it was real; he only knew he'd never felt like that with anyone else.

However, her damn father and his constant snide remarks about how Miles would never fit in with their *kind*, whatever that meant, haunted his soul. In the end, he ended up hurting Trixi, and she deserved better than that.

"Don't you have anything to say to that?" Emmerson asked softly.

"Not really." Miles ran his fingers through his thick hair. "Only, I can't deny what you're saying."

"You've got to stop this kind of thinking, especially since I believe this entire conversation started off about you wanting advice about Liberty."

Before Miles could respond to that jump in topic, Rumor showed up with a few appetizers for the table.

"I thought you boys might be hungry." She placed a platter of Safe Harbor Café's finest sampler on the table. She leaned over and kissed her husband's cheek.

"What about you, babe?" Emmerson asked. "Want anything off this tray?"

Her face went even whiter, if that was possible. "I couldn't, even though I want to. But then I'd be you-know-where and that's not fun here at work."

Emmerson sighed. "We won't be much longer. I promise."

"Take your time, honey. You're the only table I need to worry about. Susie has the rest." Rumor turned and left Miles and Emmerson alone.

Miles took an onion ring and plopped it in his mouth. He really wasn't all that hungry, but he took the time to collect his thoughts. Emmerson wasn't usually so forthcoming with his thoughts.

Or his advice.

He often tiptoed around the topics, choosing his words carefully.

But not this time.

Actually, ever since he fell in love with Rumor, Emmerson not only had a spring in his step, but he had a new confidence.

Miles liked it.

Even in this situation.

A few minutes of silence ticked by after Rumor left Miles alone with his brother.

Emmerson nibbled at the food and drank his coffee, waiting patiently for Miles to say something, only Miles wasn't even sure where to begin.

"I'm supposed to have an official date with Liberty tomorrow. But after meddling between her and Gabriel, I'm not even sure it's going to happen. Only, I was too stupid to know I was getting between her and her brother until it was too late."

"Bullshit," Emmerson said. "You did what you always do. You listened and then responded. That's your superpower. But it's also one of your greatest weaknesses because the reality is, when you care about something or someone, you do it with all your heart. It's why when Trixi got involved with that asshole, you stepped in and helped. You might not like Trixi that way anymore, but you still give a shit."

"That guy was a prick," Miles muttered. "I don't want to talk about Trixi. That's over. I don't know what to do about Liberty. I'm drowning in the deep end and I don't know what to do. I like this chick and she's making me crazy."

Emmerson lifted his mug. "Welcome to the *fall hard and fast* club. It kind of sucks in the beginning, but once you get to the other side, it's fucking wonderful."

"Sometimes you are absolutely no flipping help at all."

Emmerson laughed. "Look, little brother." He tapped his temple. "Do yourself a favor and get out of your head. Stop analyzing everything. Whatever you meddled in, apologize and then don't do it again, unless you have to when it comes to Charlie. I don't know if you've had the chance to talk with Rhett today, but I guess he found a few blemishes that are cause for more concern."

"I'm meeting him at my house before work tomorrow."

"Depending on how Rumor is feeling in the morning, I'll try to be there. I'd like to hear what Rhett has found."

"Morning sickness that bad?"

"I feel so bad for her because it lasts all fucking day." Emmerson rubbed his chin. "The moment she blinks open her eyes, she's making a beeline for the bathroom. She can't even keep a cracker down and it gets worse as the day progresses. Technically, she called in sick today, but Lucy Ann needed someone for the dinner shift, so Rumor has tried to muddle through, but she's gotten sick three times being here. Until we figure this out, she's told Lucy Ann she can't work." Emmerson slumped his shoulders. "In one week, she's lost eight pounds."

"She's so tiny as it is."

"Tell me something I don't know. She literally has no appetite. She tries to eat, but food is not her friend right now."

"She needs the calories for the baby," Miles said.

"We both know that, which is why we're bringing this up with the doc. She tries to be brave and act like she's not scared over it, but this isn't normal morning sickness. We've talked to every woman in this family who has had a baby and they all agree that this is something more. Maybe that kind of morning sickness that needs special attention."

Miles could see the worry etched in his brother's furrowed brow. "You're doing all the right things. You'll get a handle on this and Rumor and the baby are going to be just fine."

Just then, Rumor appeared at the table with a tear rolling down her cheek. "Emmerson," she said softly. "I'm spotting. I think we need to go to the hospital."

Miles was on his feet just as fast as Emmerson.

"I'll be right behind you," Miles said.

"That's not necessary." Emmerson looped his arm around his wife.

"Necessary or not, it's not up for discussion." Miles never knew a time in his life where he couldn't count on his brothers to be there for him and he wasn't about to let his brother sit in a hospital while he paced the walls worrying about his wife and child.

9

———

*L*iberty sat at the kitchen table and stared at her little brother, wondering what the hell was going on in that brain of his. He could process information, although sometimes it got jumbled through emotions he couldn't handle. He could learn certain tasks, which he'd proven tenfold working with Miles. Gabriel thrived in that environment.

But the one thing Gabriel couldn't do was deal with the harsh realities of the world, deep-seated wounds, and the emotions they stirred.

And she just dumped a world of hurt on the man.

"Gabriel," she whispered. "Are you okay?"

He rocked back and forth, picking at his thumb. "Yes," he said.

"That's all you have to say about what I just told you about Charlie?"

"It's the opposite of what he says." Gabriel rocked faster. He rubbed his hands on his shorts. His gaze shifted around the room but never landed on her. At least he hadn't bolted. After one fight she'd had with him, he took off. He'd been missing for an entire night. That had been the worst day of her life.

Maybe even worse than losing her baby.

Gabriel was her world. He grounded her in ways no one could understand.

"I told you the truth," she said.

"Is it possible that you're wrong?"

"No, Gabriel. I'm sorry. But I'm not wrong." Using a word like gaslighting might not be appropriate, but that's what Charlie had done to both of them. "When I first found out Charlie had been with another woman, I wanted to believe it wouldn't happen again. I desperately wanted our marriage to work. It was for all the wrong reasons because I didn't love him, but I did want to trust him, for both our sakes. However, Charlie kept lying to me and I turned a blind eye to it."

"Not about that. I believe you when you say Charlie wasn't faithful." Gabriel nodded. "I'm talking about the baby."

She took Gabriel's hands. "I didn't fall down the stairs. Charlie pushed me. I just couldn't bring myself to tell anyone the truth. I wanted to grieve, and then I wanted to get out. The whole thing was just so…" She wiped her tears away. "I'm sorry."

Gabriel jerked his hands away and abruptly stood. He stomped his feet and clenched his fists. "I can't believe that. Charlie was heartbroken. I watched him cry over that baby and you pushed him away. You wouldn't even let him hold her."

"That's not true," Liberty said with her heart in her toes. "You were there at the hospital with me. You never left my side and Charlie never once came. I didn't tell him he couldn't."

"That's not what he says. Nor his parents. Are they lying too? Why would they do that?"

"They wanted to control me and they did that through you. Making you believe I was to blame was one way to keep me there. But I was so miserable. Charlie wasn't good to me and I couldn't stay a second longer. Not after what he did."

"Sometimes you can be so selfish," Gabriel said. "I'm going to go work on the golf cart. Miles said I can do that whenever I want. He gave me the code to his garage."

Before she could say a single word, Gabriel was marching his grown ass out the door and across the yards.

Fucking wonderful.

But the truth was out. That was something. Gabriel would come to accept it soon enough.

She hoped.

Grabbing the bottle of bourbon and a glass, she made her way to the front porch. Part of her was concerned Gabriel might run. He'd done it before and he didn't have too many places to go in this town. More than likely if he did take off, he'd call Charlie.

At least in his present state of mind.

The second reason she went outside was she hoped she'd see Miles. She'd been hard on him and she wanted to rectify that before their date.

She found it a little odd and unsettling that she wanted this date so badly with Miles.

But it was the one thing she could call her own.

———

Miles sat in the waiting room of the hospital in the wing for high-risk pregnancies. He didn't understand why they had checked Rumor into the ER, then they moved her there immediately, but what the hell did he know about babies?

Okay, he knew a little. He babysat all the time for his brothers and their kids.

But he knew jack shit about this part.

Emmerson strolled through the glass doors with his face whiter than Rumor's.

Fuck. That couldn't be a good sign.

"I need to sit down," Emmerson said as he ran a hand over the scruff on his face, holding a small piece of paper clenched between his fingers in his other hand.

They'd been at the hospital for two hours. They

had hooked Rumor up to fluids and something to give her the nutrition she was sorely lacking. Then it became a waiting game for the doctor to arrive so they could do some ultrasound thing. Once the doc showed up, they kicked Miles out of the room.

That had been thirty minutes ago.

"I don't know what to say. Sorry doesn't seem to cut it right about now." Miles shifted, placed a hand on his brother's shoulder, and squeezed. He couldn't imagine what Emmerson was feeling. Or Rumor. The twitch in Miles' heart over the loss stung worse than a bullet.

"I'm in shock."

"I would be too," Miles said. "I know how much you wanted this."

Emmerson chuckled. "You don't understand."

Miles figured he deserved that because he didn't, so he chose not to say anything, but he was taken aback by Emmerson's response.

"Here. This says it better. Besides, I don't think I can say it out loud yet." Emmerson handed the piece of paper to Miles.

Miles held it up toward the ceiling and stared at a gray, black, and white image. "Dude, I'm sorry. But I have absolutely no idea what I'm looking at."

"This doesn't run in either family, so it's not like we'd ever expect it or even think about the possibility."

Miles brought the image closer. Damn thing

meant nothing to him. "I know you're hurting. I'm not going to say all the usual things about trying—"

"Give me that thing." Emmerson yanked the paper from his hands and shoved it in his face, pointing. "See that blob right there?"

"Yeah."

"And then that one right there?" Emmerson tapped his finger.

"Um, yeah. But I don't know what it is. Is there something wrong? Did the doctors find something? Is Rumor going to be okay?"

"Once she stops swearing at me, she'll be fine." He shook his head. "Two fucking heartbeats. Two fucking babies. Twins. Goddamned twins. My wife produced two eggs and I fertilized both of them. Fraternal freaking twins, which I guess does kind of make this my fault. Two kids at one time. How the hell am I going to do that? I was freaking out over having one child. Now I'm going to have two at once. And the doctor said Rumor has to stay in the hospital for a day or two while he figures out this morning sickness shit. Not necessarily from being pregnant with two babies." Emmerson talked so fast that Miles couldn't get in a word, but he didn't even try.

He just sat there and stared at the image of two new little Kirbys and smiled.

"You're going to be a great dad." He slapped Emmerson on the back. "You and Rumor got this.

And you've got all of us to… sit back, watch, and laugh our asses off while you try to navigate it."

"You're a dick, you know that?" Emmerson dropped his head back and lifted his hand, holding up two fingers, wiggling them. "Of all the things I thought could be happening tonight, finding out I was going to have twins was not one of them."

"Sweetest damn surprise." Miles chuckled.

"Yeah. It kind of is." Emmerson turned his head. "Thanks for being here for us. It means a lot. But you can go now. Rumor is half-asleep and Lord knows she needs it. I'm going to go home, change my clothes, and get a few things for her. Looks like I'm sleeping in this damn hospital again for the next couple of nights."

"Call me if you need anything at all."

"You know I will." Emmerson jumped to his feet. "Mom already knows. She heard we were here and called right before I came out to tell you, so I'm sure the whole family knows by now. I told her to tell them to communicate when everyone comes to visit. I don't want Rumor to get overwhelmed, but I do want everyone to come."

"We'll do what we always do and make a sched-ule." Miles gave his brother a big bro hug. "I've got a dumb question, though."

"Yeah. What's that?"

"Will these babies be identical?"

Emmerson laughed. "Thank God, no. Fraternal

means two different eggs and sperm completely. For all we know, we're having one of each."

"Are you going to find out?"

"We sure are." Emmerson nodded. "Now get the fuck out of here and make things right with Liberty."

"I'll try." Miles turned and made his way to the elevators. Hopefully it wasn't too late for a nightcap.

## 10

The night sky filled with a million stars and normally, Liberty would love to sit there and count them. But not tonight. There were too many other things on her mind and every time she tried to clear it, her brain filled with all her problems and bad decisions.

She checked her watch. It was a little past ten and Gabriel still hadn't emerged from Miles' garage. Thankfully, he'd left his phone on the kitchen table, so she knew he wasn't texting or calling Charlie.

But that meant he was in there stewing in his thoughts, not even communicating with Miles.

Where the hell was that man anyway?

Since she'd known Miles, she'd learned he was a creature of habit. More so than most people. He got up early every day. Even on those days he wasn't working. He didn't stay out late, if he went out at all.

When he did venture out after work, it was with his family. For a man who was known as a ladies' man, he didn't act like one.

When he'd raced home a couple of hours ago and hopped into his truck, he hadn't had time to talk. He mumbled something about Emmerson needing him, but that was it. He did, however, take the time to spend five minutes with Gabriel.

Miles was always good about stuff like that.

Lights cut through the dark street. The sound of his powerful engine roared as he pulled into his driveway. He waved as he got out of the pickup before disappearing into his garage.

She sighed.

It was possible she might not see him tonight and she didn't have the bandwidth or the energy to chase him down.

Her cell buzzed.

She lifted it and tapped the screen.

**Lucy Ann:** *Is there any chance we can move your shifts around? Rumor is in the hospital. She's fine. The babies… yup… twins… are fine. But she's out of commission for a little while. Maybe even the entire pregnancy. I need someone on nights more than I do mornings. I know that might not be possible. But I'm asking everyone.*

Liberty thought about that for a moment.

**Liberty:** *I could swing tomorrow night. The rest of this week might be tough unless I find something for Gabriel to do.*

**Lucy Ann:** *I just heard back that I have all nights*

*covered this week except tomorrow. If you could swing that, I'd been forever grateful. We can then all regroup and figure out a schedule that works for everyone.*

**Liberty:** *I can make that work.*

Liberty glanced toward Miles' place. Still no movement from inside the garage. She decided on texting Miles.

**Liberty:** *Can you come over for a second? I need to talk with you.*

She set her phone on the small table and contemplated texting Rumor. No. It was too late. Whatever happened that sent her to the hospital, Liberty would find out soon enough.

Twins. Wow. That was some big news.

Five minutes ticked by before Miles emerged.

No Gabriel.

"Hey." Miles climbed the stairs to her porch and took a load off. He stretched out his legs and smiled. "Emmerson is going to have twins."

"I heard."

Miles arched his brow. "That news traveled fast. I wonder if that means I get to be a godfather twice."

"That's a question for your brother and his wife," Liberty said. "I need to ask a favor. Lucy Ann needs me to cover Rumor's shift tomorrow night."

He scowled. "That means you're canceling our date. That I don't like. I was looking forward to it, but we can reschedule and I'll just go fishing with Gabriel and my brothers."

"Thank you for understanding."

"I have a feeling that Rumor won't be working anymore."

"That's what Lucy Ann expects, but I don't know if I can swing the dinner shifts because of Gabriel. With Charlie hanging around, I don't trust he won't just show up."

"Any evening you have to work, he can hang out with me. It's not a problem." Miles shifted, catching her gaze. "My mother's husband has a niece, Stephanie, who's on the spectrum. She lives in the next town over and they'd like to introduce her to Gabriel."

"I think that would be nice. He had a couple of friends back in Palm Beach who were like him and he enjoyed hanging out with them. He just didn't like going to the center. It made him feel different."

"I can understand that." Miles laughed. "When I was little and the teachers would pull me out of class, it always made me feel like shit." He tapped his finger on her knee. "Gabriel doesn't want to come home tonight."

"Excuse me?" She sat up taller.

"I found him half-asleep in the golf cart, wrapped in a sleeping bag he found in my garage."

"Jesus," she whispered. "He was just going to stay there until you got home?"

"He wanted to text me, but he said he left his cell

at home and he didn't want to come back and get it, figuring you'd never let him leave again."

"What else did he tell you?"

"Not much, honestly. Only that he's confused and he doesn't know what to believe."

"He should believe his sister." She sighed. So many mistakes. Too many wrong decisions. She couldn't go back in time and make different ones. All she could do was try to ease the pain. But with Gabriel, it wasn't going to be easy. She'd hurt him in the worst way by lying. She'd broken his trust and it was going to take a miracle to get it back.

Miles took her hand and kissed it. "I know I don't have to tell you this, but his emotions don't connect to his thoughts the same way ours do. The truth to him is black and white. There are no gray areas and your reality has a shit ton of gray. You were damned if you were honest. And damned if you weren't."

"Thank you, I think."

"Seriously. If you had told Gabriel the truth as things happened, he would have crawled into a hole. He wouldn't have been able to cope in that environment." Miles arched a brow. "Unless you had left."

"Right. The judgment for staying with the prick is rearing its ugly head."

"That's not what I'm doing. It's just, once you made the choice to stay with Charlie after the first affair, telling Gabriel wouldn't have been a good idea. Telling him the truth about how Charlie pushed you down the stairs would have caused more harm than good, unless you told the cops and pressed charges, but even if you did that, you would have had to take some precautions to help Gabriel through it." He raised his hand. "I've watched too many of my sisters-in-law be in shitty situations where they had to make interesting choices in order to survive. That's what you did. I don't have to agree with them. But now that Gabriel knows the truth, he needs a moment to process the new information and that means he has to face a different kind of betrayal."

"Sometimes I really resent you," she whispered. "But I don't think it's a good idea for Gabriel to spend the night at your house. He doesn't do well with change and he could wake in the middle of the night and freak out."

"You'll be happy to know that I told him hiding out at my place wasn't the manly thing to do and that he should come home. He's contemplating that right now."

"Thank you." She nodded. "And I am sorry about canceling our date. I too was looking forward to it."

"We'll do it the next night you're free. Actually, Steve and my mom are having his niece and family over this weekend. We could go over with Gabriel for the introduction, and if all goes well, we could bug out and have our date."

She narrowed her eyes. "Are you trying to fix up my little brother?"

"I'm not. But I can't speak for my mother." Miles laughed. "She meddles like that."

"Oh my God. That's the last thing I need."

"Autistic adults can date. Have romances." He pulled out his cell and waved it. "I googled it and there's lots of information about it."

"Trust me. I've read them, but there has always been some question about where Gabriel lands on the spectrum. He's so smart. He functions well that way. But he's like a toddler in other ways."

"Don't get mad, and I'm by no means an expert, but could some of that be because of his life circumstances?"

She nodded. "I've had that conversation with counselors. So, you're not speaking out of your ass. Our life wasn't easy. Gabriel struggled early on because our parents refused to get him the help he needed. Once they left, I felt like I was constantly playing catch up. When Charlie came into my life, Gabriel was doing really well and Charlie wasn't the prick he is now right off the bat. But Gabriel has regressed and that's on me."

"Don't do that to yourself." Miles leaned closer, brushing his lips over her mouth in a sweet, tender kiss.

The rattle of floorboards under her feet made her jerk.

She looked up.

Gabriel stood on the fourth step.

"Sorry to interrupt," he said. "I decided to come home. But that doesn't mean anything. I'm still mad. I don't know who to believe or what to think. I'm going to bed." He marched past them and opened the door, glancing over his shoulder. "You can resume the kissing." He disappeared into the house.

Miles chuckled.

"That's not funny."

He cleared his throat. "Come on, it's a little funny and I'm down for some of that."

"You're impossible."

He traced her jawline with his finger. "I'll leave if you want me to. Just say the words."

She said nothing.

Seconds later her tongue was wrapped with his in a tango. A warmth spread across her skin as she gripped his shoulders, digging her fingernails into his hard muscles.

He lifted her off the chair, tugging her to his lap.

She should protest. She should end the kiss. But all she could do was deepen it because she needed what Miles had to offer.

His hands wrapped around her body, pressing her chest firmly against his, finding every inch of her exposed skin.

No one had ever kissed her with such passion and tenderness before. It was a combination of wild abandon and sweet love.

Miles was a contradiction. He was this gentle

man. A man who had all the right words. He knew exactly what to say at the right moments. But he was also reserved with his emotions. And while he had a confident swagger, underneath all that, there was a hint of insecurity.

Trinity had shared some of where that had come from, and it made understanding him a little better.

But Liberty still didn't get it.

He cupped the back of her neck, massaging gently, then let his hand roll down the front of her chest, cupping her breast, pinching her taut nipple through her flimsy T-shirt.

She arched, moaning.

The pure pleasure of it all caught her off guard.

Sex with Charlie had become a chore. She hated it, especially after they lost their baby. She avoided it at all costs. She came up with every excuse in the book so she didn't have to do it.

But it often didn't work and she'd lie there like a lump on a log, doing her best not to feel anything, when every fiber of her being filled with shame and guilt.

"Either I should leave, or we should take this inside before one of my siblings, or worse my mother, drives by and has to arrest us for indecent exposure," Miles whispered.

Being with Miles was something she wanted. Craved. Her body demanded it, but her mind began swirling with all the reasons it wouldn't be a good idea to do it again. She decided to ignore the brain.

She stood, taking his hand, and quietly led him through the house and into her bedroom. Quickly, she closed and locked the door. She stood there, staring at Miles. "Not to sour the mood, but you have to leave after we're done. I can't have Gabriel finding you here in the morning. Seeing us kiss is one thing, but—"

Miles pressed his finger over lips. "If you don't want anything more to happen, I'm okay with that."

"I wouldn't have taken you into my bedroom if I didn't." She lifted her shirt over her head and tossed it to the side.

His eyes grew wide as his gaze dropped to her pathetic excuse for a bra. He lifted his hands and reached behind her, unhooking the article and letting it fall to her feet. He dotted kisses on her neck, shoulders, and then he took one of her nipples into his mouth.

She gasped in pure delight.

She ran her fingers through his hair, pulling him closer to her chest as she let out a soft moan. His hands explored her curves, sending shivers down her spine as he kissed his way down her stomach. She could feel the heat between them, igniting a fire that consumed all rational thought.

He unsnapped the button of her jean shorts and slowly lowered the zipper, rolling them over her hips and yanking them and her panties to her ankles.

As he caressed her skin with a featherlight touch, she melted into his caress, completely lost in the moment. His every kiss fueled her passion, driving her to the brink of ecstasy.

He laid her back on the bed and pulled his shirt over his head before lifting her leg and kissing her ankle. Then her knee. He licked his way up her thigh, all the way gazing into her eyes.

With a tender smile, he whispered, "I want to make you feel so good that you don't want me to leave, even though I know I have to."

She bit her lip, a mix of anticipation and desire washing over her. "You already have," she murmured, her breath hitched as he slowly traced her belly button with his finger.

Inch by inch, he ascended closer to her core, his touch sending ripples of pleasure coursing through her body. She clutched the sheets, staring at him with a fierce intensity, her whole world narrowed down to the sensations he was creating in this moment.

Finally, he reached his destination. Miles' lips met her skin, gentle yet insistent, awakening a hunger inside her she didn't know was there. His tongue danced around her folds. "You taste like heaven."

She moaned softly, both in pleasure and shock. This was something she had never experienced before, and it was unlike anything she could have ever imagined. He explored her most intimate parts, sending waves of pleasure crashing through her body.

She writhed beneath him, her hips arching to meet his touch.

Miles continued to please her, his tongue delving deeper, drawing out sounds from her that she didn't even know she was capable of. He knew just what to do to make her feel alive, to make her feel desired and wanted.

She gripped the sheets tighter, her breath coming in short gasps as he continued to tease her, driving her closer to the edge of ecstasy. She could feel the heat building inside her, the tension coiling like a snake, ready to strike.

"Please," she begged, her voice hoarse with longing. "Please, I need you." As soon as the words escaped her lips, an orgasm tore through her system. She jerked and quivered. It was like a volcano had erupted, shooting hot lava everywhere. She couldn't catch her breath. Her heart beat so fast.

"That was beautiful." He kissed her midriff and stood, shedding his slacks. He stood before her, gloriously naked. Reaching inside his pants pocket, he took out his wallet and a condom.

She watched in awe as he covered himself before settling back down between her legs.

Nothing in her life had ever felt so good. So perfect. So right.

As Miles entered her, she gasped at the sensation, feeling every inch of him as they became one. Their bodies moved in rhythm, a sinuous dance of desire and passion. Her hands explored his back, nails digging into his skin, leaving red marks as a testament to the intensity of her pleasure.

Her mind hazy with lust, she felt like she was floating, her body lifted off the bed by the sheer force of their lovemaking. Miles' movements were precise and deliberate, as if he was trying to extract every last ounce of pleasure from her. And she was more than willing to give it to him.

She moaned loudly, her voice echoing off the walls as their bodies punished each other with a ferocity that bordered on pain. But it was a good pain, a necessary pain, one that only heightened the sensation of their union.

She felt herself nearing the edge again, her orgasm building like a tempest inside her, threatening to overwhelm her completely. But Miles was relentless, his thrusts growing deeper and harder, pushing her closer to the brink.

"Oh, God, yes," she begged, her voice a ragged whisper.

He complied, increasing the rhythm of their coupling, each stroke more intense than the last. The sound of their bodies slapping together filled the room, punctuated by her gasps and a series of sharp, high-pitched cries.

Miles leaned down, his breath hot against her ear. "That's it, sweetheart. Let yourself go."

The words were like a match to gasoline, igniting

her fiery passion and sending her spiraling over the edge. The orgasm that erupted within her was all-consuming, a maelstrom of pleasure and pain that engulfed her entire being. Her body convulsed, her soft moans filling the room as she rode the waves of ecstasy.

Miles continued to move inside her, his thrusts becoming more erratic, driven by the force of her climax.

With a final, powerful surge, he let go, his body shuddering as he spilled himself inside her. The sensation was indescribable, filling her with a warmth that spread through her entire body.

They lay there, panting, spent, their bodies still entwined. The room fell silent, except for the sound of their breathing slowing in tandem. Each breath brought her closer to earth, grounding her in the reality of what had just happened.

As they finally disentangled themselves, Miles pulled her close, his arms wrapping around her. She nestled into him and closed her eyes tight.

He kissed her temple. "I hope you're not going to kick me out of this bed right now, because that might crush me."

She chuckled. "No. But you can't stay too long. I'm afraid if we fall asleep, we won't wake up before Gabriel does. Please don't take that personally."

"I'm not." He kissed her temple. "How about we watch a little TV, and then I'll leave." He reached across the bed and found the remote, pointing at the television.

"Sounds like a plan."

She had no idea what this was or where it would lead, but she didn't believe it could be forever. No matter how much Miles gave of himself, he still held back a piece. It wasn't that she believed he didn't trust her with his whole self.

But as she draped her arm and leg over his body, she couldn't deny the distance that suddenly grew between them. It wasn't as if he physically pushed her away, because he didn't. But his touch was different. It wasn't as intimate. And while she had no real basis other than maybe a woman's intuition, she got the distinct impression that Miles had already left her bed.

She ran her finger up the center of his chest. "A penny for your thoughts."

He chuckled. "Not much going on in my brain," he said softly, staring at the TV, which played some old sitcom. He held the remote in one hand, while the other rested on her shoulder, but his fingers didn't dance across her skin.

"I don't believe that." She rested her chin on his pec. Trinity had warned that he would pull away and that when he did, she should call him on it. But did she really know him well enough to do that? If she wanted this to be anything other than one or two rolls in the hay, she certainly needed to work on communication.

And so did he.

Especially when he was the one who had mentioned doing the whole dating thing right. Well, since they were two sexual experiences in and no dates, that was out the window.

"I'm tired. It's been a long day. Perhaps it's time for me to go." He lifted the covers, but she grabbed his arm.

"Not so fast." She sat up, pulling the sheet across her body. She tapped his temple. "Not until you tell me what just happened because you went from sixty to zero in about two seconds flat."

"It's late and we both agreed it's not a good idea—"

"I know what we agreed to, but you don't get to give me a couple of the best orgasms I've ever had and then close up on me like a fucking brick wall. Now either you tell me what's going on, or I'll tell you what I believe is your problem."

He jerked his head, arching a brow. "This should be interesting."

"You really want to go that route?"

"I don't want to have this conversation at all, but I will admit to being intrigued." He sat up taller. "I'm listening."

She tucked her hair behind her ears, which let the sheet fall to her waist.

"Um. Nope. Can't concentrate when I'm staring at those." He waved his finger.

"For fuck's sake." She twisted, making sure everything was covered. "We just had an incredible moment. Granted, we don't owe each other anything. We haven't even gone out on a date." She cocked her head. "But don't act like that was just sex or that I'm another notch on your bedpost. Because you've been coming after me hard for the last month. So, to pull away from me after really good fucking sex, well, that's just mean."

"First, that's not how I view this." He furrowed his brow. "And I resent the idea that you think I'm using you that way."

"I didn't say that you were. The key word there is you were acting that way. Not that you were doing it." She leaned over and covered his mouth. "Your real problem is that you like me."

He jerked his head. "Of course I do."

"Yeah, well, when you get into that weird zone where liking someone is real, you get in your head and do to yourself exactly what you accuse me of doing to Gabriel." She poked his biceps.

"And what is that?"

"Treat yourself like a damn child incapable of doing anything for yourself." She lowered her chin. "I'm not asking you for anything and I know all you're asking of me is a chance. I'm willing to give it, but now that you have what you want, you've already got one foot out that door." She pointed. "All because you have some ridiculous idea in your head that you're not smart enough, which is about the dumbest thing I've ever heard."

He stared at her with unblinking eyes. His lips parted and let out a long slow breath. "And who in my family have we been talking to?"

"Tell me I'm wrong," she said, folding her arms.

His chest rose up and down with each breath he took. Three minutes ticked by and he didn't say a single word.

And his silence spoke volumes.

"Maybe it is time for you to go," she whispered.

"No. You're right." He cupped her face and kissed her tenderly. Lovingly. It wasn't the same confident Miles that took her to bed. It was a better version. A vulnerable version.

And she liked this man even more.

"I'm sorry. I can't help it sometimes." He ran his thumb across her cheek.

"Just like you're not Charlie, I'm not Trixi or her family," she said. "What you see or what you believe others see as limitations, I see as part of who you are. Watching how you deal with Gabriel has shown me just how wrong I've been with some of the ways in which I deal with him all out of loving him. I see how your family is with you, but what you seem to fail to understand is that the only person holding you back is you."

"Now you sound like my father." He took her hand and kissed her palm. "But these learning disabilities do hold me back. They have my entire life. Accepting them hasn't been an easy road for me, but I wasn't given much of a choice. I know I'm good at what I do, but it's everything else in life that's a struggle."

She sighed. "We all have struggles, Miles. You keep telling me that about Gabriel. Why can't you see it for yourself or understand how fucking smart and intuitive you are? I care about you, not whether or not you have to listen to an audiobook versus reading it for book club."

"I don't do book clubs." He chuckled.

She slapped his shoulder. "You know what I mean."

"I do." He nodded. "And I hear your point. Trust me. You're not the first person to give me this lecture, though you're the first woman to."

"So, are you going to be fully present so we can go back to a real after-sex cuddle before you do the walk of shame in the middle of the night?"

"I can handle that."

"Good." She eased into his arms, and he held her as close as he could, his fingers dancing across her skin as they watched some old show.

She yawned.

"You're good for my soul, Liberty."

Closing her eyes, she let her body relax and enjoyed the moment. She had no idea what the future held or even if she and Miles would last longer than a hot minute.

But it didn't matter.

They needed each other to heal old wounds. She would help him get past the shit talk he told himself and he would help her with her new beginning.

What happened after that would be left to the stars.

## 11

Miles blinked his eyes open.

This was not his bed. Or his bedroom.

Liberty's body was sprawled out next to him with her hair pooled over his chest. It was still dark, so maybe it wasn't morning yet. He reached for his phone.

Fuck. It was five.

"Liberty," he whispered, shaking her shoulder. "We fucked up."

"What?" She brushed her hair from her face and blinked. "Oh, no. What are you still doing here?"

"No time to get into that discussion. Just go see if Gabriel is awake. If he's not, I'll sneak out as fast as I can." He jumped from the bed and hiked up his jeans. "I'm sorry."

"You should be." She fumbled out of bed and snagged her robe.

"Hey. You fell asleep too."

"Maybe. But you were the one… never mind. I'll be right back." She ducked out of the bedroom.

Miles couldn't remember a time when he slept past four. It was like he had a fucking internal clock and his eyes automatically opened at that time. He would always try to sleep at least one more hour and sometimes he'd be able to doze off here and there. But not always.

Last night, he'd slept like a fucking baby.

Never happened when he shared a bed with a lady.

He liked his space and inevitably, a woman always invaded it, reminding him he wasn't alone. And Liberty was right. He always had one foot out the door long before anything got too complicated. He wouldn't dare call Liberty a complication. Far from it. If anything, her presence helped him make sense of his life. As if all the pieces of a puzzle fell into place. Only, last night, when his emotions got the better of him, he got scared.

More frightened than he'd ever been, even when he'd been with Trixi and that relationship had freaked him the fuck out.

Liberty tiptoed back into her room. "He's not up yet. Now go." She gave him a good shove.

"Okey dokey. But not before this." He cupped her face and planted a wet one on her lips.

"Stop that." She pushed him away.

He cocked his head.

"Not because I don't like it." She pointed toward the door with a sleepy smile.

"Fair enough." Miles tossed his shirt over his shoulder and snagged his boots. He raced out of the bedroom and through the front door, skidding to a stop at the top of the steps. All the air in his lungs flew out like a jet taking flight. What started out as a semi-fantastic morning turned to shit at the sight of Charlie and his fucking stupid Porsche.

Miles dropped his boots to the wood floor and leaned against the railing while he watched Charlie slip from the driver's seat. A million and one things floated through his mind, including punching the asshole in the nose.

But his mother hated it when it was his fist that went flying first.

For now, he'd see what this jerk-off had to say before reaching for the phone and letting the family full of cops and lawyers deal with the situation. Hopefully, Gabriel and Liberty would stay tucked inside.

"Isn't this an interesting surprise," Charlie said.

"The sun isn't even up yet. Not to mention you're not supposed to anywhere near Liberty." Miles raked his fingers through his hair. The way his blood boiled, he knew he wouldn't be able to keep his cool. Time to call in the cavalry, only when he went to pull his cell from his back pocket, it wasn't there.

Fuck. He'd left it in the bedroom.

"I'm not here to see her." Charlie inched closer. "I came for Gabriel."

"That's not happening either. Kindly leave."

"Sorry. The only person who's going to tell me to take a hike is Gabriel. Not some stupid-ass grease money Liberty's made her pet project." Charlie laughed. "So typical of that woman."

"What the hell is that supposed to mean?"

"Before we got together and when she was in her rebellious stage, she always went for your kind. Guys with long hair, tattoos, and no direction in life. When I first started courting her, she was dating this guy who ran fishing charters." He shrugged. "He wasn't a bad guy, just didn't have any ambition." Charlie tapped his temple. "Not too bright either. Lucky for her, I took her away from having to struggle paycheck to paycheck." He waved his hand out in front of him and sighed. "Only, now she's back at it again and slumming it with the likes of you. It won't last. She'll get bored and come home where she belongs."

A switch went off in Miles' brain. The same one that landed him in the back of Nathan's patrol car when Trixi's father and brother got in his face.

He took the steps two at time with his fists clutched at his sides. His shirt flew off his shoulder and landed on the grass.

"Miles," Liberty yelled, yanking his mind—and body—out of the insanity that would surely land him in his mother's jail cell.

He stopped dead in his tracks, six inches from Charlie's face. "If she hadn't come out, you'd be face down in the pavement," Miles whispered. He took a step back, shaking out his hands, but no fucking way would he turn his back to this asshole.

"You forgot your cell," Liberty said with a shaky voice. "Charlie, if you don't leave, I will call the police. Don't make me do that. Gabriel doesn't need the drama."

Charlie raised his hands, showing his palms. "I didn't come to see you. I'm here because Gabriel asked me to meet him for breakfast." Charlie looked Miles up and down. "Although, I'm not sure Gabriel would appreciate this idiot sneaking out of your bedroom, like the lowlife he is. Gabriel doesn't like secrets or surprises." Charlie lowered his chin. "And this one is beneath even you."

"How dare you." Liberty leaped off the porch.

Miles curled his arms around her waist, stopping her from lunging at Charlie. She'd been the voice of reason with him five minutes ago, now it was his turn.

"Don't you lecture me on my brother." She tried to shove Miles out of the way. "And seriously? Gabriel isn't even up yet. I don't know what you think you're accomplishing by showing up here this early. I doubt he'd contact you. And do you know why?

Because I told him the truth. Every last ugly bit of it and honestly, it felt fucking good to finally be honest with my brother. For him to know what a prick you are."

The sound of the front door screeching across the floorboards caught Miles' attention. He turned his head. Shit.

"Me? Are you kidding. You're a liar. I can't believe you'd do that to your brother," Charlie said with a shitty grin. He knew Gabriel was standing there and he played into it.

Gabriel stepped outside with tears in his eyes. How much he'd heard, Miles had no idea, but Charlie certainly wanted his side to be the one Gabriel believed.

"The only mistake I made was not telling Gabriel the truth sooner," Liberty said.

"Liberty." Miles took her by the shoulders. "Gabriel is standing on the porch."

She spun on her heel. "Shit."

Gabriel hugged himself and rocked back and forth, mumbling a few choice words.

"I'm so sorry you had to hear that." Liberty raced to her brother.

"Me too, especially all the lies your sister just tossed around about me. I can't believe you, Liberty. I don't know what you told Gabriel, but lying to make me out to be the bad guy instead of taking responsibility because you're mad at me for some ridiculous reason isn't right." Charlie inched closer. "Gabriel, I'm sorry she's putting you in the middle of all this."

"You shut the fuck up." Miles stepped in front of Charlie. "One phone call and you'll be in cuffs in four minutes. Up to you."

"I. Want. The. Fighting. To stop," Gabriel yelled.

"I'm going to speak to him and you're not going to stop me." Charlie glared, taking one small step to the side. "Hey, Gabriel. Why don't you come down here and we go for a drive."

"No!" Gabriel stomped his foot. "I asked you to wait until I texted, but you showed up early. I don't like that. I only wanted to ask you a couple of questions, but now I don't need to. I know the answers." He raced down the steps in his pajamas and barefoot and ran toward Miles' house. He punched his finger against the garage code until the motor roared to life.

"What the fuck is he doing?" Charlie narrowed his stare.

"None of your business." Miles swallowed as he watched the garage door go back down with Gabriel safely tucked away inside. "In three seconds I'm calling the cops."

"You mean your family," Charlie mumbled. "Liberty, this isn't over. I don't know what kind of bullshit you're feeding Gabriel, but it's got to stop. It's not good for him and it's not doing you any favors." Charlie climbed behind the steering wheel and backed out of the driveway.

"Well, that was a shitshow." Miles smiled and waved to one of the neighbors who had stepped outside with the ruse of drinking their morning coffee. Two others were pretending to look for the newspaper. One even opened the mailbox, which was almost laughable. He let out a long breath and strolled across the lawn. "What do you want to do about Gabriel?"

"I need to go talk with him. Alone." She leaned against the railing. "I seriously thought you were going to deck Charlie."

"If you hadn't called out my name, I would have." He kissed her cheek.

"Why?"

"I didn't like how he talked about you."

"If you're referring to him all but calling me a slut, that's stupid and not worth getting into a fistfight over."

Miles rubbed the back of his neck. "Maybe, but let's not forget I had to step between you and him too."

"I wouldn't hit him. I wouldn't have even gotten in his face. But I did want to see his reaction to me responding differently."

"I don't know. I stepped in front of you when you were only five feet away."

"Yeah," she said. "And by that time your back was to him and he was grinning like the devil." She wrapped her arms around her middle and shivered. "Right about then, I would have halted in my tracks.

He was baiting me. He wanted me to come at him. He wanted to have to put his hands on me all in the name of calming me down. I wasn't going to fall for it. But you let him get in your head. That wasn't about me or defending my honor. That was Charlie hitting the right nerve." She lowered her chin. "He had to have been checking into your past to learn that would have set you off. But how did he know you were here?"

"Gabriel?" Miles cocked a brow.

"It's possible, but the only way for me to find out is to have a conversation with him. Mind opening up your garage for me?"

"I'll make us some coffee while you two chat." He pressed his hand on the small of her back and guided her toward his house. He punched the code on the keypad and waited patiently while the door lifted.

But Gabriel wasn't in the garage.

"The door to the house is open. He must be inside." Miles took her by the hand and stepped into the kitchen. "Gabriel, where are you?" Miles' heart dropped to his stomach like a brick when he saw the back sliders were open.

Liberty raced through the open doors. "Gabriel!" She stood on the back deck and did a three-sixty. "He's not out here."

Miles tapped his cell. "Dammit. He turned his tracking off."

"You're tracking my little brother?" She glared. "He barely agreed to let me do that."

"He said I could and for the record, he can track me too." Miles let out a long breath as he pulled up his mother's contact information. He put his phone on speaker. It rang once.

"Hey, Miles. This is early, even for you. What's up?"

"Charlie showed up Liberty's this morning. He left, but Gabriel took off out my back door. On foot. In his pajamas. He couldn't have gone far, but with Charlie around, it's got me worried. I'm getting in my truck now to go look, but I wouldn't mind all hands on deck."

"Sending a text to Nathan, Emmett, and Chris right now. I'll be out the door in five. We'll find him," his mom said.

"Thanks." He tapped the red button.

"I've got to go put some clothes on." Liberty raced past him in a flash.

"I'll meet you by my truck." He closed the back door and snagged his keys. His boots and shirt were outside.

What a fucking nightmare.

He tried calling Gabriel, but it went straight to voicemail.

Shit.

The poor man. His entire world had been turned upside down and Miles was partly responsible for that.

Something he couldn't deny.

For all he knew, Gabriel had known he'd spent the night and it had upset him to the point he reached out to Charlie. If anything happened to Gabriel, Miles would never forgive himself.

---

Liberty slipped from the passenger seat of Miles' truck. Tears stung her eyes. It had been hours since her brother had gone missing and there was absolutely no sign of him anywhere. He hadn't shown up at any of Miles' brothers' homes.

Or at the auto shop.

Or the park.

Or the diner.

No one had seen him.

And Miles' mother didn't think it was a good idea for her to go to Charlie's house or his place of business and ask him where the fuck her little brother was. Rebecca believed that was a police matter.

Miles agreed.

Liberty wasn't sure if she was on that same page. There was a small part of her that couldn't believe Charlie would do a single thing to hurt Gabriel. Only, Charlie had proven time after time that he was a manipulative son of a bitch who would do anything to get what he wanted.

And for whatever reason, he wanted her.

But she couldn't understand why and pitting Gabriel against her wasn't the way to do it. Not anymore.

"Maybe he came home." Miles wrapped his arm around her shoulders.

She shrugged it off. "I've tried texting and calling. He's not answering. He hasn't done that in a long time." She jogged up the steps of her porch and unlocked her front door. "Gabriel? Are you in here?" She searched every inch of her house, but there was no sign of her brother.

He wasn't even in his room playing video games, which often calmed his nerves. She ran her fingers over her brother's unmade bed. Gabriel was a creature of habit. He liked things to be neat and orderly. He never left his room without pulling his comforter over the mattress. She tugged it toward the pillows and something fell to the floor.

His phone.

She reached over and picked it up. That cell was his lifeline. He liked to have it with him at all times. Mostly because he liked to text her about everything he learned at the shop. Sometimes he texted her fifteen or twenty times a day. It warmed her heart.

But then there was Charlie. Cutting her brother off from him had been difficult, but necessary.

She barreled down the stairs, wondering where the hell Miles had gone since he hadn't followed her inside.

She opened the front door and slumped into one of the chairs.

Miles emerged from his garage. "He's not at my place." He held his cell in his hands, tapping away on his screen. "My mom and Nathan should be at Charlie's house and Emmett and Chris texted that they just pulled into his place of business. We should know more about that within the half hour."

"I found Gabriel's phone. He didn't take it with him." She set the cell on the table. "It's locked and I don't know the passcode."

Miles lifted it and ran his finger over the top. "I can see all our calls and texts, but there are some here from a number I don't recognize." He held it up. "Is this Charlie?"

She glanced at it. "Yeah. That's him."

"We'll need to give this to my mom," Miles said. "I doubt she'll be able to legally hack into it, but she might let Rhett give it a whirl unofficially, and then maybe we can read the communication."

"We've only lived here for two and a half months. He doesn't know his way around that well. Only through town and maybe to Emmerson's place." She hugged her knees. "I should have never told him the truth."

Miles sat down next to her and took her hand.

"Don't touch me." She jerked it away.

He raised his hands. "I'm only trying to help."

"If you had left last night, none of this would have

happened." She dropped her head to her knees and groaned. Deep down she didn't mean those words, but she needed to blame someone and Miles was right there. Only he didn't really deserve it. "I'm sorry," she whispered. "I didn't mean that."

"No. It's okay. I'm sure me strolling outside half-naked didn't help matters and I did lose my shit when your ex-husband called me a grease monkey, stupid, and your pet project all in one breath."

"He's an asshole and none of those things are true, except maybe one, but I don't see how that's an insult. You're the best at what you do and there's nothing wrong with your profession. Charlie doesn't know shit about cars. Hell, he can't even change a fucking tire." She dropped her feet to the floor. "Gabriel knew my old phone number by heart. And he is good with numbers, so I feel confident he knows this one. But if he's frightened, people won't know how to respond to him."

"He couldn't have gotten far on foot," Miles said. "Half the town is looking for him. We will find him."

"What the hell did he want to ask Charlie anyway and what did he mean when he said he had the answers now?"

"I don't pretend to know Gabriel better than you, but if I had to guess, he wanted to catch Charlie in a lie. He wanted to take what you told him and try to see how Charlie would spin it. Gabriel has always been on your side and I think perhaps he saw through his shit."

"Gabriel has never been on my side. Not when it came to me losing the baby. That one he has always blamed on me. And I let him." She swiped at her cheeks and stood. "I can't sit here and do nothing. I need to go back out there and look for him."

"We're going to wait right here until after someone in my family has questioned Charlie. If that turns up nothing, then we can talk about going back out, but we should consider being here in case he comes home. I'd hate for him to return and no one be here."

"We could take turns."

"My only worry about that would be if Charlie showed up and leaving you alone to deal with him. I wouldn't want that for you."

She opened her mouth but it was cut short by a ringtone.

"It's my mom." Miles tapped the screen. "Hey, Mom. What happened at Charlie's place?"

"He says he didn't know anything about Gabriel being missing and that he was on the way to a listing. Not much else I can do without probable cause, which I don't have, but I'm working on it and we'll keep an eye on him. I'll be in touch."

"Thanks, Ma. I appreciate it." Miles scooted his chair closer. "I know it feels like we're not doing anything by sitting here and waiting. But if Gabriel does come home, I think you should be here when he does and I don't feel right about leaving you."

Tentatively, she reached her hand out and palmed his unshaven cheek. She wanted to lean on him for support. God knew she needed someone right now. Charlie had never really been there for her, even when things between them had been decent. He only cared about himself and how he looked.

"I need to tell you something, but I'm afraid it will piss you off." He kissed the inside of her palm.

She cocked her head. "Whatever it is, better to lay it on me than beat around the bush or lie to me."

"I would never do the latter," he said. "My brother Rhett is on his way over. I was supposed to meet with him this morning about something he found regarding Charlie."

"What did he find? Is it bad and why was he digging?"

"I asked him to and I can't imagine it's good," Miles said. "He wanted to meet with me alone, but under the circumstances, I've told him that whatever he has, you need to know."

"Thank you for not keeping it from me." She stared out across the street. A few neighbors strolled by with their flyers in their hands, holding them, nodding. No words were spoken, nor were they needed. The fact that everyone on her street kept wandering the town in search of Gabriel made all the difference in the world.

But it didn't change the fact that it was approaching ten in the morning and her brother was still missing.

"But why would you dig into Charlie's background?" she asked.

"I don't trust him and there are a couple of things that don't add up in my mixed-up brain."

"I'm going to make you start paying me a dollar every time you put yourself down." She tucked her hair behind her ears. "There's nothing wrong with the way your mind works. Only with how it processes words on the page."

He blinked. "Trust me. There's a lot wrong with how I handle information, but that's not the point. I've heard you say you don't understand why Charlie wants you back after everything you've been through. Him cheating. The baby. Even the differences in financial situations. It got me thinking that there's always a reason for this shit and it's often never what it appears to be on the surface." He lowered his chin. "Like him telling everyone he loves you and Gabriel because we both know that's bullshit."

"You got that right, but if I wasn't so interested in what your brother dug up, I'd be pissed."

A very large, fancy dark SUV rolled to a stop in front of her house. Rhett, with his man bun, eased from the driver's seat. He and Miles looked a lot alike. If Miles let his hair grow, they'd look like twins. Rhett tucked a folder under his arm and strolled across the front lawn. "Any news?"

"Not yet." Miles stood and gave his brother a manly hug.

"I'm so sorry, Liberty." Rhett leaned over and kissed her cheek. "We've got everyone combing the streets. Some friends of mine are walking the campsites and local parks, even out by where I live. We're not going to leave any stone unturned."

"I appreciate that." She did her best to compose herself. "Miles tells me you have some kind of dirt on my ex-husband."

"Dirt is one way of describing it and something tells me you're not going to like any of it." Rhett pulled up a chair and set the folder on the table, flipping it open. "I learned a lot about Charlie, but three disturbing facts stick out. The first one is his grandparents placed a contingency on his trust and his inheritance. As in he doesn't get it unless he's married. There's also a timeline on having an heir and that caps out at forty." He handed her a couple sheets of paper. She glanced at one before waving it at Miles.

Miles took it but didn't even glance at it. He tucked it back in the folder, keeping his gaze focused on his brother.

"He'll be forty next year," she whispered. "Is something like that even legal?"

"It's called conditional gifting and rich people do it all the time," Miles said. "Trixi's father has threatened her with that her entire life. When we were dating, he cut her off completely and told her if she stayed with me, she'd be cut out of the will. But even now, she has to do certain things to get her money when that crazy bastard dies. One of them is never marry a grease monkey like me. Not even if he's rich."

Liberty smacked her head. "What the hell is wrong with being a mechanic? It's an honest profession and everyone needs a good one. Jesus, I don't even know where that dip thingy is to check my oil."

"I'll show you that, and other things, because everyone should have basic knowledge." Miles took her hand. "So, what you're telling us is that within this next year, Charlie not only needs to be married, but he has to be expecting a child in order for his grandparents to give him money?"

"His grandfather died six years ago," Liberty said. "And his grammy has been sick these last few months. She's not expected to live much longer."

"Were you close to either of them?"

"They were always kind to me. Nicer than anyone else. Even though they had the same expectations of me when it came to fitting in. And they enjoyed Gabriel's company to the point they sought him out, not the other way around." Liberty sighed. "Charlie's grandparents were friendly with my parents. My folks were closer to them than they were Charlie's parents. Though they all had business dealings together. My dad always enjoyed working with Old Man Livingston. Sometimes, when my dad and I weren't fighting, he'd talk about how fun it was to work with him, but he didn't trust Oswald. Once Gabriel was diagnosed, my dad worked even more and he stopped talking to me about it less."

"That brings me to the second disturbing fact." Rhett pulled out a piece of paper and handed it to her.

"What am I looking at?" She stared at the document.

The names on the page tormented her soul.

Harvey and Robin Blue.

"What do my parents have to do with any of this?" Her fingers trembled as images of her childhood flashed in front of her eyes. When she'd been a little girl, she'd been the apple of her father's eye. Every night, he'd tuck her in with a special *Daddy* story. He'd done the same for Gabriel, where her mother was more interested in the *ladies who lunch* and all the gossip. She would dress her children as if they were trophies, only bringing them out on special occasions.

Until Gabriel had been diagnosed.

That's when her father began drinking at night and her mom continued on as if nothing had changed.

"I didn't think too much about the business connection between the Livingstons and your parents," Rhett said. "However, the second Gabriel went missing this morning, something tickled my brain and I went back to the paperwork."

"My father was in real estate for many years, among other things. Merging his company with Livingston's was a no-brainer. It made them the biggest, most successful company in all of Florida, but he completely sold it to Charlie's father when he disappeared, freeing him up to do whatever he wanted."

"That's actually not true." Rhett tapped his finger on the document. "As I went down a very strange rabbit hole, I found something odd. One is that your father is still very much a part of that company. As a matter of fact, he owns seventy percent, where the Livingstons only own thirty and he's opened offices up in South and North Carolina."

"You've got to be fucking kidding me." Liberty drew the paper closer, trying to make sense of the information. "How is that possible? Why would they let people think they walked… assholes. They did it because they wanted a clean slate, away from their disabled child."

"I'm still combing through all the paperwork," Rhett said. "But it appears that the Livingstons were facing financial ruin before your father stepped in."

"It was Charlie's dad who helped me get a job when my parents left. He was part owner in that restaurant," she muttered. "I can't believe they were struggling. They've never wanted for anything."

"Charlie's grandparents have money. But Oswald does not. And what little he earns from Livingston Development, he's mismanaged. So has Charlie," Rhett said. "One more thing you should know about your parents before I continue with some other information is that they divorced three years ago." Rhett arched a brow.

"No way. My mother would never agree to that. My recollection of their fights is that she signed a prenup and would get next to nothing," Liberty said softly. "Unless my dad cheated."

"I haven't dug into that situation, but I will." Rhett waved his hand over the folder. "Back to all of this, because I couldn't leave well enough alone." Rhett leaned back. "Your father, up until you divorced Charlie, has been sending your ex-husband a nice big fat check."

"Why the fuck would he do that?" She blinked.

"I don't know for sure," Rhett said.

"But I could take a wild guess," Miles mumbled. "Do you have the contracts for the business merger? And how it's amortized for new offices through all the business partners? And is Charlie a full partner or an employee?"

"I need you to slow down." She squeezed Miles' leg. "I'm not following what any of this could mean and I'm staring at a piece of paper that should explain it, but I don't understand it. How can you follow any of it and you haven't even looked at it?"

"I don't know anything." Miles snatched it from her fingers and placed it in the folder. "I'm just asking my brother the questions as they fill my brain based on the information he's given me."

Rhett sighed, shaking his head. "Normally, I'd say my little brother is being humble, but in reality, he's just being a dumb fuck."

"I resent that," Miles said.

"Really? Good. Because we get tired of you thinking and believing you're as stupid as a rock, when you process verbal information faster than a speeding bullet. Even I can't do that, and I have the IQ of a fucking damn genius."

"Not the time or place for this." Miles glared. "Answer my questions about the contracts and shit."

"I've got them, but all I've been able to do is skim them. Shelby is reading them as we speak."

Liberty shifted her gaze from Rhett to Miles. "I want to know what you're thinking and I want to know now."

"It's a whole lot of conjecture based in little fact." Miles pointed toward his brother. "He's read the paperwork and his wife—"

"Cut the bullshit," Liberty said. "You have a sixth sense about this shit just like you do cars."

"Damn, I knew I liked this chick, but now I think

I'm kind of a little in love with her," Rhett said with a chuckle. "Go on, tell her."

Miles pinched the bridge of his nose. "There are a few problems with my theory. The first one is if Harvey wanted his children to be taken care of financially, why didn't the money start rolling in to help her before she got married. Especially if this was all a setup before they left Palm Beach."

"I'm going to fucking kill the lot of them." Liberty bolted to her feet, knocking over the table. She paced in front of the steps. "Are you trying to tell me that my parents bribed Charlie and his family into…" She let the words trail off as she stared at Miles.

"What is it?" He raced to her side, wrapping his loving, kind, warm arms around her trembling body.

"What was the exact amount of those deposits?" She held Miles' stare.

"Rhett?" Miles glanced over his shoulder.

"Fifty thousand a month," Rhett said.

"That dirty rat," she mumbled, covering her face. "And my father, why couldn't he just tell me?"

"Okay, I'm not following."

She swiped at her cheeks. "When my folks left, my dad did leave me with some money to start. I took it. I'm not a fool. But a couple of months later, fifty grand mysteriously appeared in my bank account. Charlie was already sniffing around and I told him about it and the idiot that I was, let him look into it for me. He told me it was a mistake. That the bank accidentally deposited someone else's money into my account. He gave me something to sign." She covered her eyes.

"Hey. You were young. Your parents had just abandoned you with a ten-year-old boy to take care of. Charlie was a family friend and you did what any of us would have done. You trusted him." Miles kissed her temple.

"You know what that means, though, right, little brother?" Rhett asked with an arched brow.

"Yeah. That there's an account somewhere with the name Liberty Livingston on it that her father's been depositing money in that he thinks is going to his son and daughter." Miles took her by the shoulders. "I need to call your father. You don't have to be present if you don't want to, but we need answers that only he can give and while it might not help us find Gabriel right now, it's going to help us nail that fucking ex-husband of yours to the wall."

"You're not going to call him." Liberty squared her shoulders. "I am."

## 12

*L*iberty wished it wasn't so early in the day so she could have a glass of bourbon. She swallowed. Hard. The last time she'd spoken to her father had been three days before he up and left. He'd been sitting in his den, drinking scotch, and playing a game of chess with Gabriel.

His father could have a fair amount of patience for Gabriel, even if he didn't understand the child.

Their mother, on the other hand, didn't give one shit. She couldn't be bothered. At least their dad spent time with Gabriel and that's what made this whole thing even worse.

Gabriel cried at night, not for his mother, but for his dad.

"Are you sure you don't want me to do this?" Miles tapped her phone on the center of the island in her kitchen. "I'm happy to talk to him for you."

"I know you are and I appreciate the support. I really do. But I have to do this."

"All right." Miles squeezed her biceps. "Do you want me to stay with you or step outside?"

"Stay." She found her father's contact information that Rhett had sent her and she hit the call button. It went to voicemail. She should have known her dad wouldn't take a call from someone he didn't know. "Hey, Dad." God, that felt weird to say. "It's Liberty. I need to speak with you. It's urgent. Please call me. Thanks." She tapped the screen.

No sooner did she open her mouth to say something than her cell vibrated.

"Looks like he's willing to have a conversation." Miles kissed her cheek. "If you need me to jump in, just say the word."

She sucked in a deep breath and let it out slowly. "Hi, Dad," she said softly.

"Wow. I can't believe I'm speaking to you." Her father's voice bellowed across the air like a freight train. "Are you okay? Is Gabriel okay?"

"I'm surprised you even care enough to ask," she mumbled.

"I guess I deserve that," he said. "Why are you calling?"

"The money."

"After all these years you want to ask me about that now? I think my guilt money speaks for itself and you've been using it, so I'm grateful you accepted it."

She squeezed her eyes, blinking out a tear. "That's just it, Dad. Until an hour ago, I didn't know that money existed."

"What! That fucking son of a bitch. I told your mother that man was no better than his father and certainly not the man his grandfather was. I'll deal with that little shit and make sure you and Gabriel get what you need. I know you left Charlie and he has no right to that money. It's for you to take care of Gabriel."

Miles rested his hand on her back and ran his fingers up and down her spine, giving her the strength she needed to continue.

"I don't even know what to say about the money. And I have even more questions about why you didn't tell me you were doing it," she said.

"I left you a note... shit. I bet your damn mother destroyed it, making sure you didn't get that too. I'm sorry," her dad whispered. "You probably don't know this, but your mom and I divorced and that money is part of the reason it happened. When she found out I was giving it to you, she lost her shit. But we were done anyway. Too much had gone down and for the last three years I have been grappling with whether or not I should reach out, but I figured you'd never forgive me and I know Gabriel. It wouldn't be good for him."

"You don't know shit about your son and you lost

the right to know anything the day you walked out of our lives."

Silence on the other end of the line.

And she had no idea where to go with the conversation anymore.

Miles cleared his throat. "Excuse me, sir," Miles said. "You don't know me, but my name is Miles Kirby. I'm a friend of Liberty's. I'm helping her with a situation that involves her ex-husband. We need to know where you've been sending that money since the divorce because she hasn't been getting it."

"That's easy," her dad said. "But I don't understand. I got an email from Liberty with the new banking information."

"What email? I never sent you an email, Dad. Ever. I haven't communicated with you since three days before you left."

"That's not true. I have the emails from you informing me of your connection to Charlie and new routing numbers." Her father let out a dry laugh. "When I got wind of the separation, I called Charlie's parents and they told me that you two were working things out, but I heard through old friends that wasn't the case. I started following it myself and I emailed you through the chain from when you first got together with that little prick. That's when I got the new routing numbers."

"Sir, can you tell us what email addy it came from

and then forward me those emails? Because they didn't come from Liberty," Miles said.

"Sure, but I want to know what the fuck is going on because I get the impression this is more than that jerk stealing from my kids."

Liberty sat up taller and tucked her hair behind her ears, holding Miles' gaze.

He tapped the mute button. "Tell your dad whatever you're comfortable with."

"I don't know if I believe him," she whispered. "I want to. My memories of him aren't as bad as my mother, but he still abandoned us."

"Let's at least find out why he controls that business." Miles tapped the screen, not giving her a chance to respond.

But she trusted Miles, so she'd let him control this situation.

She nodded.

"Sir, before we get into some of the things going on, we have a few more questions," Miles said. "Why did you merge with Livingston Development?"

"Jesus Christ." Her father let out a long breath. "How do you know about that?"

"Does it matter, Daddy? Could you for once in your fucking life be honest and answer the damn question." Fuck it. Liberty pushed from the counter and strolled to the liquor cabinet where she pulled out a bottle of bourbon and poured two fingers. She tossed back a big gulp.

"That's the Liberty I remember." Her father laughed. It was a hearty chuckle and one that reminded her of the good times.

That just pissed her off.

"There's a little backstory to this tale, so you're going to have to give me a minute," her dad said. "When Oswald took over the company, it was booming. But he destroyed it. He took a little healthy competition that his grandfather and my old man thrived in and turned it into this cutthroat atmosphere until his company was on the brink of destruction. When I took over for my dad, Old Man Livingston and I had a great relationship. It didn't matter that we were bidding against each other half the time; we made each other better and we loved every second of the battle. Win or lose, it was a thrilling game. But Oswald only cared about winning. At all costs. He didn't care about the customer."

"Oh, and you did?" Liberty's words were laced with a heavy dose of sarcasm.

"I very much did, but your mother had different ideas and let's just say I allowed myself to get lost in that shuffle. We had you, and then Gabriel came along and our marriage was shit, but that's a different story," her dad said. "Old Man Livingston came to me when he found out his company was on the verge of falling apart. Oswald had run the ship aground and he needed help. I was planning on leaving your mother and taking you kids with me."

"Excuse me?" Liberty stared at the phone and blinked. "I don't believe that for one second."

"It was in the note I left that you never got, and again in these emails that you say never reached you,'" her father said. "But your mother had an ace up her sleeve that stopped me dead in my tracks. So, instead of leaving her, I quietly absorbed Livingston Development as a favor to Old Man Livingston, but there was a caveat to it."

"And what was that?" Miles asked.

"He was to help you get a job, find good housing, and keep a watchful eye over you and Gabriel," her dad said. "I knew Charlie had eyes for you, but I didn't know he was going to come after you so quickly, and never in a million years did I believe you'd marry him, especially since I was giving you that money. I figured it would be enough for you to finish college and help Gabriel with whatever he needed." A loud thud echoed across the air. "I can't believe he's been stealing that money. When I agreed to the new office in Lighthouse Cove, I was told it was because you two were working on things and it was so he could be closer to you and Gabriel. I guess that's not true."

"No, Dad. It's not," Liberty said. "Charlie's a snake. A criminal. And I want him out of my life."

"I'll do what I can to help you with that, starting with making sure Miles gets all the information he needs from me. I don't want to close down that office, but I can make sure Charlie isn't in it."

"That would helpful, but I don't want you to pull that trigger just yet," Miles said.

"Why not?" her dad asked.

"Because Gabriel is missing and I'm beginning to wonder if Charlie might have something to do with that." Miles took the glass from her hand and set it aside. Then he wrapped his arm around her waist, holding her close.

He always knew exactly what she needed. He was intuitive that way and she adored him for it.

"My God, Liberty. Why didn't you lead with that? I'll fly down there as soon as I can," her father said.

"That's not going to help," Liberty whispered. "And I'm not sure I want to see you."

"I can't say that I blame you. I wouldn't want to see me either." Her dad let out an audible sigh. "But I can't sit here and do nothing. I've been wallowing in self-pity for years. You may never forgive me. I'm not sure I can forgive myself. And I get there might be no hope for me and Gabriel. You say I don't know him, but I did—do—love him. I might have fucked up in the worst way, but I'm not as heartless as you think. We can save that one for your mother."

"You're seriously going to toss her under the bus, as if she's the only one to blame in this fucking mess." Liberty pushed from Miles' embrace and picked up the phone. She glared at it as if she could shoot daggers across the cell waves.

"No. Trust me. I take full responsibility for my

actions and right now, I will do whatever it takes to make sure Charlie gets what he deserves for stealing your money and for whatever else that shithead did to you. As far as your mother goes, well, once I send those emails to your friend, you can decide for yourself," her dad said. "It's strange. I thought you hated me because of the truth. Now I find out you simply didn't know."

"I hate you for abandoning us."

"Well, there's that," her dad said. "I'll be there in a few hours. I will keep a safe distance from Gabriel when you find him. I will respect that. But now that this conversation has been had, once you read that email, I'd like to talk with you about it because it matters to me."

"Dad, I don't want to—"

"I'll text you when I land." The phone went dead.

"Fuck," she mumbled. "He's the last person I want to see."

Miles raised his cell. "My mom is on her way here. Let's hear what she has to say, and then hopefully your dad will have emailed me and you can read it to me."

"How about you read it first." She sighed. "And tell me what it all means."

"I can ask my mom to do it, but this is where my learning disability bites me in the ass." He pressed his finger over her lips. "I'm not hiding behind it or using it as an excuse. Reading is really problematic. I can do diagrams. I can do text to speech. But reading looks like a foreign language."

She palmed the side of his face. "This is the part of you that I adore."

"What does that mean?"

"You didn't say you wouldn't understand it." She leaned in and pressed her lips over his mouth. "You're one of the smartest men in any room. Once you allow yourself to go with your instincts, there's nothing that you can't do. You know who to trust and who to lean on and you do it with ease." She tapped his temple. "When you get out of your head."

"You're good for a man's ego." He pressed his hand on the small of her back. "Come on. My mom's here."

Miles leaned against his mother's patrol car and folded his arms. "So, that's it. You're just going to do nothing."

"I didn't say that, Miles, and don't give me that sourpuss face. I hate it." His mom glared. "We questioned Charlie and he acted as if Gabriel being missing was brand-new information. Do I personally believe him? No. I don't. I think he's lying through his fucking teeth. But I have no evidence to go on. I've got no probable cause to do anything. Following him would be harassment, which is why Rhett's on that.

Once he gives me something that I can legally move on, I will. Outside of that, everyone is turning this town upside down looking for Gabriel."

"But you believe the same thing that I do." Miles sighed.

"The only thing that makes sense is that Charlie has him in that big house of his." His mom cocked a brow. "Why else wouldn't he invite me in? Hell, he wouldn't even let me have a glass of water when I asked. He gave me some bullshit excuse that he had a showing he needed to get to."

"And did he leave the same time as you?" Miles asked.

"Oh, he did." His mother laughed, shaking her head. "But according to Rhett, he didn't go to any showing. He went and picked up a to-go order from the café. Two cheeseburgers and two fries." She waggled her finger. "You know as well as I do that's not enough for me to go asking for a search warrant or go back and bang on his door right away. I will, in an hour or so, under the pretense of doing another sweep."

"That's just fucking weird he'd pick up food. For two. And not immediately go looking for Gabriel, someone he claims to care so much about." Miles glanced toward the house. "He did text Liberty telling her he was doing all that he could, but it's bullshit. I've asked Dad to look over all the banking documents after Liberty has read them. That might give you what you need as far as a search warrant, or even an arrest warrant."

Movement near the thick brush in the backyards caught Miles' attention. Whatever it was, it was large enough to stir the bushes, making them rustle and snap.

And then Gabriel appeared in the clearing.

Still in his pajamas.

Still barefoot.

"Miles!" Gabriel flapped his arms wide as he raced between the houses, his body covered in dirt and mud.

"I'll go get Liberty," his mother whispered.

Gabriel flung himself at Miles like a toddler.

Miles widened his stance, digging his heels into the ground as he braced for impact. "I got you, buddy." He wrapped his arms around Gabriel.

"I walked the whole way." Gabriel sniffled, nuzzling his face into Miles' neck, holding on to him with brute force. "I snuck out when he wasn't looking, and then I walked along the beach, staying in the bushes for as long as I could until I got to town."

"That was real smart." A million things went through Miles' mind, but it was more important to make Gabriel feel safe and loved than to bombard him with a million questions about what happened. But he did need to know a few things.

Miles guided Gabriel toward the front porch. "I know you've been through a lot today and are just glad to be home, but I have to know. Did Charlie hurt you in anyway?"

"No," Gabriel said with a strong voice.

"Oh my God. Gabriel. Are you okay?" Liberty came rushing through the door.

Gabriel hugged his sister and burst out crying like a little baby.

Both brother and sister crumpled to the floor, where Liberty cradled her brother's head in her lap, stroking her fingers through his hair and kissing his temple while the man sobbed.

And sobbed.

"He should be checked out by a doctor," Miles' mother whispered.

"It might be a little too much to take him anywhere right now and he says he wasn't hurt," Miles said.

"What if we called Jameson and he and a paramedic come over?" his mother asked. "Just to be on the safe side."

Miles glanced at Liberty.

She nodded.

"It's okay. It's all going to be okay," Liberty said softly.

Miles wiped the tear that escaped his eye. He leaned against the railing and glanced between Liberty and his mother.

"I know you don't want me to do this now, but I

need some answers before I go after Charlie," his mom said.

"Oh, trust me, I get it." Miles nodded. "We just need to give him a moment."

Gabriel scooted to a sitting position. He sucked in a deep breath. His lower lip quivered. "I'm so sorry I went with him."

"Gabriel, do you remember my mom?" Miles sat on the floor. He didn't bother to look Gabriel in the eye. He knew he wouldn't get that in return. He did, however, motion to his mom to join them on the steps.

Which she did.

Gabriel nodded.

"I know she's kind of scary in her uniform." Miles chuckled. "She still frightens me sometimes when she wears it, but she's one of the good guys and she needs to know what happened. Do you think you can tell her?"

"I was so mad." Gabriel made his hands into tight fists and slammed them on his legs. "I could tell Charlie was lying because his story always changed. But I was also so angry at Liberty for treating me like a child. As if I wasn't man enough to handle the truth." He swiped at his eyes. "I wanted some time to think. I was just going to walk to the shop and maybe work on that old engine you let me tinker with in the back room. But then I saw Charlie and I wanted to confront him. I wanted to tell him I believed my sister and that he was the liar. He told me he wanted to tell me the whole truth. Everything. Not the bits and pieces and he took me to his house, but he lied again."

"About what?" Miles' mom asked.

"My sister." Gabriel smacked the side of his head. "He stuck with his version of what happened, but then added that Liberty was using it to try to take his money. I knew she'd never do that. When I told him I wanted to go home, he said he'd call my sister, but then he lied again. He told me that Liberty was too busy with Miles to come get me. That she didn't have time for me and that he would take care of me."

"Oh, Gabriel. No one, not even Miles, would ever come between us." Liberty cupped her brother's face. "I love you and you're the most important person in the world to me."

"I know that," Gabriel said matter-of-factly. "But Charlie knew that Miles spent that night and he tried to tell me that Miles didn't want to be burdened with having to deal with someone like me. He said that Liberty agreed. He even tried to tell me that Liberty had begged him to take me off her hands and that's why he moved here, to make sure I was being properly taken care of. When he saw Miles, he thought maybe it was time to take legal action."

"Jesus, he said all that?" Miles did his best to rein in his rage. This wasn't about him or his feelings. This was about Gabriel and what had just happened to him and how they were all going to help him through it. "How did you respond to all that?"

"I knew Charlie was lying. I just didn't know why. I still don't." Gabriel sniffled. "I was scared. My heart hurt and all I could do was sit in the chair and rock. I tried to sort through my thoughts, but it was hard. Then the doorbell rang and Charlie made me go into the den. But I heard what you said." Gabriel pointed to Miles' mother. "That I was missing. That everyone was out looking for me. I tried to get out of that room to tell you I was right there. But Charlie had locked the door."

"That fucking asshole," Liberty muttered.

"What happened next?" his mother asked with her cell in her hands.

"When I heard him drive away, I climbed out the window and came home." Gabriel rested his head on Liberty's shoulder.

Jameson's SUV rolled to a stop in front of Liberty's house. A buddy of his, Riley, a paramedic from the firehouse, slipped from the passenger seat carrying a bag and strolled toward the house.

"Gabriel, I'm sorry this happened to you," his mother said. "Thank you for telling me what happened. I know it wasn't easy and that you had considered Charlie your friend. But what he did was wrong and now I need to handle that." His mother tapped her fingers on her cell. "Do you understand that?"

"Yes, ma'am. I do." Gabriel nodded. "Will he go to jail?"

"I want you to know I don't enjoy arresting anyone," his mother said in a soft tone. "But yes, mostly likely he will and not just for what he did to you."

"I'm tired. Can I go play some video games?" Gabriel lifted his chin and looked at Liberty.

"Sweetheart, Jameson and his friend here would like to check you over. Just to make sure you're really okay." Liberty palmed her brother's cheek. "Let them listen to your heart. Check your blood pressure. All those things. Do it for me so I will feel better."

"Okay." Gabriel nodded.

"How about we go inside to the family room," Jameson said. "Gabriel, this is my good friend Riley. He's what we call an EMT and he's one of the best."

Gabriel stood. "Do you drive the ambulance?"

Riley chuckled. "I do."

"Saving people is a cool and important job." Gabriel glanced over his shoulder as he stood by the front door. "Is Miles going to spend the night? Because maybe he should until Charlie is caught." Gabriel shrugged. "And I'd be okay if he did even after that happened." He turned and shuffled his dirty feet into the house.

"I'd say out of the mouths of babes, but that is a grown-ass man." His mother laughed. "I've got all I need to go back and make an arrest for kidnapping. But it's a weak case. And as far as what I know about Charlie pushing Liberty down the stairs when she lost her baby, well, that's a case of he said-she said. I don't know if the DA will touch that one without more proof. I'd like to nail him for it because that's about one of the cruelest things I've ever heard and I've seen a lot during my time as a cop." She held up her hand. "Find me a smoking gun in that paperwork Liberty's father sent over." His mother wrapped her arms around Liberty. "I'm going to nail your ex-husband to the wall. It's going to be my last case, and then I'm going to retire. I'm too old for this shit. But I want you to know that I'm not resting until Charlie's behind bars for a very long fucking time. I don't want that man to ever hurt you or Gabriel again."

"I don't know how to thank you and all of your family."

His mother smiled. "Just keep reminding my son he's good enough."

Miles shook his head and watched his mom climb into her patrol car and drive away.

"She's an interesting character." Liberty leaned into his body and rested her head on his shoulder. "I can't believe Gabriel walked all the way home. That's like six miles."

"It won't be too long before the news of his return hits Charlie's ears." Miles wrapped his arm around Liberty. "He's either going to come straight here or make a beeline for Palm Beach, or worse, the airport."

She groaned. "And my father will be here in a couple of hours."

"Come on. Let's go check on Gabriel and then read those emails. My mom will need that information and I'd rather pawn it off on my dad before he even gets here. You're as exhausted as Gabriel. I want you to nap before you see your dad."

"That actually sounds amazing."

Miles helped her to her feet and yanked her to his chest. "I want you to know that I care about you. A lot. It's not a fleeting moment. Or a fling that will burn out in a few weeks. Whatever this is, I've never felt it before and I have no intention of going anywhere."

"I know. But one thing at a time. Let's deal with Charlie. Then my dad." She sighed. "And then maybe we can finally go out on that date."

13

*L*iberty sat in front of her laptop at the kitchen table. Gabriel had passed out minutes after Jameson and his friend left. Gabriel had been a little dehydrated but, otherwise, physically fine.

But the emotional scars would last a lifetime.

Miles stood behind her with his hands firmly planted on her shoulders, massaging gently. Somehow, he'd become her rock. There was no way she'd be able to handle any of this without his kindness or support.

Her fingers hovered over the keyboard. She stared at her father's email. The first one had an attachment from an email she used when she first met Charlie. But he talked her into getting a new one. A Livingston one.

The second email had an attachment from that email.

"Here goes nothing." She opened the email and then the attachment.

"*Dad,*" she began reading out loud.

"*I appreciate the money. Thank you. However, you should know I'm dating Charlie Livingston and things are serious. Interesting turn of events, isn't it? Anyway, that doesn't change what you did and I certainly don't forgive you. Call me selfish, but I want that money. For Gabriel. However, I've moved and changed banks. Here is the new routing numbers. Please start making those monthly payments there. And know the money is going to take care of Gabriel. His education. His needs.*

*Liberty.*"

"I never fucking wrote that." She let out a long breath. "It doesn't even sound like me."

"Nope. It does not."

"How could my father even think it was or that I'd need his money if I was marrying that fucking asshole?"

"Guilt makes people do and believe strange things. Trust me. We watched my parents behave in all sorts of weird ways while they lied to us about Jameson's paternity." Miles waved his finger over the screen. "Keep reading."

"*Liberty,*

*Wow. I'm not even sure what to say. Congratulations. Although, I'm shocked that you would have any kind of romantic involvement with Charlie Livingston. Besides you not wanting anything to do with that kind of lifestyle, the boy is a bit of an idiot. I can't tell you how many times his grandfather or I have had to bail him out of a bad business decision, but maybe he's grown up. It can happen. But I doubt it when it comes to Charlie because, well, you may not know this, but I own the majority of Livingston Development. Very long story that I'm not sure you're ready for and if you were, I'd keep that information to yourself. Unless you need it to protect yourself and Gabriel. The money will start showing up in the new bank account next month. I'm sorry about what I did. But the note explained it all. If you ever want to talk about that, I'm here.*

*No matter what, I'll always be your dad where it mattered.*"

"What the fuck does that mean?" She glanced over her shoulder. As if being her father was more important in certain areas of her life than others.

"Unfortunately, I believe I know the answer," Miles mumbled, pulling up a chair. "Is there any more in that email chain?"

"Just one stating that I will no longer be using that addy and directing him to a new one."

"All right, open the next one." Miles waved his hand over the keyboard.

She inhaled sharply, clicking on the next email from her father.

*"My Dearest Liberty,*

*It's been a long time since you've reached out. I don't blame you. I wouldn't want to speak to me either after everything. I guess I'm just surprised that you didn't have questions for me after what I told you in that note. I recently learned that you're getting a divorce from Charlie, so I'd like to know where to send the money. It's for you and Gabriel, no one else. Again, if you ever want to talk about things, let me know.*

*Oh, your mother and I are divorced.*

*Your dad. Where it matters."*

She scrolled down the attachment.

*"Dad,*

*Here's the new account. I would have reached out with that when it was time. Outside of you doing what is financially right, we have nothing to say to one another.*

*Liberty."*

"Well, outside of one word, that does sound like me." She let out a dry chuckle. "There's one more response from my father and then nothing."

Miles scooted closer. "This isn't going to be easier to hear."

"Yeah. I've gathered. I'm just not sure what he's going to say, except I know I'm not going to like it." She tapped the arrow down button.

*"Liberty,*

*You are NOT your mother's daughter. You might not be mine biologically—"*

Liberty covered her mouth and gasped.

"You really didn't expect that?" Miles ran his hand up and down her arm.

"Absolutely not and it makes all of this even more confusing."

Miles kissed her temple. "My gut tells me that whenever he found out, he did what he could to protect you, even if it doesn't feel that way." Miles arched a brow. "Keep reading."

She blinked. Tears filled her eyes. Of all the things she expected, this wasn't it. But Miles was right there with her and he knew. He sensed things. Even if he didn't want to believe how smart he really was, she valued his insight and would be lost without it.

*You might not be mine biologically, but I did raise you for twenty years. I was the one who drove you to school every day. I was the one who went to your tennis matches and supported you when you wanted to quit. I was the one who tucked you in at night and I was there for you in the hospital when you had your appendix out. Not your mother. Me. And I did it because I loved you. I still do and yes, I do get I had a shit way of showing it when I up and left. But understand this. I didn't leave you when you were nine and I learned you weren't mine. No. I stayed because in every way that mattered, I was your father. However, you've already heard this because you read it in that note but have chosen not to respond.*

"I never got the note, Daddy," she managed behind a guttural sob.

"Do you want to take a break?" Miles held her close. God, she'd be mad without his strength. His wisdom.

Dare she even think it?

His love.

Whatever it was, she needed Miles and she wasn't going to let go.

"No. I need to finish this." She blew out another puff of air.

*"You know what, maybe you need to hear this story again and perhaps now that I've finally left your mother, I need to tell it. So, here we go. I was going to divorce your mother when I learned she'd had an affair and that you might not be mine. I had confronted her, and she denied it all. A few months later, after I had proof of the affair and had secretly done a paternity test between you and me, I told her I was leaving her. She informed me she was pregnant with Gabriel. My heart sank. I didn't know if he was mine or not, but again, it didn't matter. I wasn't going to let her take him from me. So, I stayed in what had to be the worst marriage ever and I can only imagine what that was like for you and Gabriel. Apologizing to you now wouldn't be enough, though I am sorry.*

*Once it was clear that Gabriel was special, your mother essentially walked away from both you kids. I know that it feels like it was easy for me to do the same, but it wasn't. I made the decision to leave your mother and I was working on an exit strategy. Part of that included ripping up the proof of your paternity. I was your dad and I loved you. I wasn't going to let her take that away from me, but she won and I wasn't man enough to fight her because in a court of law, I probably would have lost Gabriel.*

*Why, you ask?*

*First things first.*

*You see, when I told her my plans, she informed me of who your biological father was and she was ready to tell you. She was ready to hurt you, to get to me. But I was willing to deal with that. I figured over time, you might want to still have a relationship with me, because it wasn't my fault for what your mother did. When I told her to go ahead and tell you, your mom went for the jugular. She told me she'd fight me for custody of Gabriel. She was technically a stay-at-home mom and I was the workaholic dad who was emotionally abusive because she'd had an affair a long time ago. That I'd never forgiven her and I abused her. I also deprived Gabriel of the love and support he needed and she had the proof. All the staff that had been fired. All lies, but the emails came from an account that had my name on it because she was that good of a manipulator.*

*I spoke to my attorney, but he told me it would be an uphill battle. That I'd have to put Gabriel through the wringer to prove I was the better parent. I didn't want to do that to him. I decided it was better for you kids to hate me and have each other than go through the mess that your mother would have done to us all.*

*But I wanted you to have the truth, which is why I left the note. I knew you'd never do anything with it because it would have hurt Gabriel. But for some reason, I don't know why, I thought maybe you might have at least spoken to me about it. Given me a little credit for trying to protect you, even if I was a dick about how I did it. Okay. There. It's out in the open. Do with it what you want. Know that I've never stopped loving you. I think about you and Gabriel every day. I get that makes up for nothing. I hope you do well without Charlie in your life. He's a jerk and you can do much better than him.*

*Love, your dad."*

"That's a lot," Miles whispered.

"There's another one, supposedly from me dated almost three months ago stating that Charlie and I were working on our fucking relationship," she said with her heart in her throat. "Charlie played my father. He manipulated both of us, driving that wedge even deeper." She pushed the computer to the side, dropped her head to the counter, and sobbed. It was guttural, out of control, and there was no stopping it. She didn't know if she felt sadness, pain, anger, or this was a simple purging of years of not knowing or understanding.

All she knew was that the man who pulled her to his chest and ran his fingers through her hair adored her more than any other human could.

Miles understood her wants, needs, and desires before she did half the time. He was the sand to her ocean.

He was hers to hold when she needed comfort and right now, she needed it more than ever.

"Let it all out, babe." Miles lifted her into his arms and carried her to the family room where he eased onto the sofa, still holding her in his lap. His hands ran up and down her arms. His lips kissed her temple. Her forehead. Her neck. He whispered kind, loving words in her ear.

There was no judgment.

No words telling her what she should or shouldn't do. He was just there.

"I don't know how to respond to any of this," she whispered.

"Do you want a little piece of advice?"

She lifted her head and stared into his soft ocean-colored eyes. "Yes."

"Don't do anything with it right now." He traced her jawline with his finger. "When Jameson found out the truth, he basically cut my mom out of his life. He barely spoke to any of us unless he had to. While he had every right to be angry, he held our mother to the fire more so than our dad, who lied to his face every day."

"But it was your mother who cheated."

Miles nodded. "However, that wasn't on Jameson. Or on us. That was between my parents. Granted, it produced a child, my brother and one of my best friends. But at the end of the day, we're all now glad it happened." Miles shifted, pulling his cell out and glancing at the screen. "Your father just rolled into town. I can tell him to meet at my house or at the café if you're not up for this." He lifted her chin. "I need to ask him some questions that might help my mother nail Charlie."

"How come we haven't heard from her yet?"

"Because she hasn't found Charlie, which makes

me nervous," Miles said. "And because she put Emmerson in a car outside your house."

"What about Rumor? Emmerson should be with his wife."

Miles palmed her cheek. "I'm sure Rumor kicked his sorry ass out of her hospital room and told him to go take care of the rest of our family."

"I'm not family," she whispered.

He chuckled. "Today, you and Gabriel are. That's how the Kirbys roll and right now, you're stuck with the lot of us." He waved the cell. "What do you want me to tell your dad?"

"To meet at your place," she said. "But I want to check on Gabriel and take a few moments alone to collect myself."

"Are you sure?" He lowered his chin. "If you change your mind and want me to handle it all, I can do that. Just text me and let me know."

"I won't back out. However, if I don't take a little time, I might come in hot and that's not going to get me any of the answers I need. Both for me and Gabriel, and for what your mom needs to make sure my asshole ex-husband goes to prison." She pushed from his warm embrace and stood. "It's time to end this madness once and for all. It's the only way I'll ever be able to stand on my own two feet."

"I'll see you shortly." Miles kissed her so sweetly she melted in his arms.

It was the kind of kiss that told a woman she

would be loved and protected for the rest of her life. It was a kiss laced with the promise of a future. A kiss filled with the truth of what real love was all about.

It was a kiss that glowed in the dark, showing her safe passage home.

***

Miles had felt like an outcast and misfit his entire life, except when he was in the auto shop. That's where he shined. He knew his way around any engine. Any vehicle. Whether that be a car, a truck, a motorcycle, or even a boat. Granted, he couldn't read an owner's manual to save his ass, but he didn't need to. Not anymore.

An engine was second nature.

It was home.

Spending time with billionaires who dealt with spreadsheets, stock quotes, and did million-dollar deals on a daily basis, well, that gave him fucking heartburn.

He popped two Tums and stared at the bottle of bourbon on his counter.

Nope. That wasn't the way to deal with this situation.

*Trust your gut. Your instincts. Once you have the information, you process it better than anyone I've met. You can debate anyone in open court if you had to. Stop the internal dialogue that plagued your childhood and dump what Trixi's father did and you will have all that you desire.*

Those were his dad's words.

*Good enough.*

His mother's words.

Whatever she meant by that.

*Flunked sophomore English twice. With the same teacher. Bombed the SATs. Won't get into college. He'd be lucky to be a garbage collector.*

Those had been his guidance counselor's words to his mother and that had been the day she agreed to let him go to trade school. No one tells her that one of her kids wasn't going to amount to much.

But she had to go and tell him to work harder. To prove that idiot wrong.

Not the right pep talk at the time.

However, thinking about it now, she was right. And he'd done it. He proved them all wrong and he'd done something he could be proud of. All those assholes who put him down now came to him when their vehicles didn't work. Or they got into a fender bender. He was the best money could buy and they all knew it.

He wasn't good enough, yet he was the best in his chosen field.

But that's when his mind went down that twisty road of not being good enough for any woman. For a family.

He tapped his chest. His heart was telling him

something else completely. Two people right now were relying on him not to fuck up.

*Ding-dong.*

Shit.

He strolled to the front of the house and pulled open the door. The man who stood before him was a little over six feet and looked almost exactly like Gabriel. It was uncanny.

"You must be Miles," Harvey Blue said. He held a dark backpack in his hand.

Miles stretched out his arm, taking Harvey's hand in a firm shake.

"Where's Liberty?" Harvey asked.

"Next door making sure Gabriel is asleep." Miles waved Harvey inside. "Can I get you a drink?"

"If you have some scotch, I'll take that on the rocks. Otherwise, a beer would do the trick."

"Follow me." Miles made his way to the kitchen and found a bottle of scotch. He poured three fingers and then went for the bourbon. He might as well join the man.

Harvey set his bag on the counter and eased onto one of the stools at the island. "My daughter has an infinity for good bourbon." He laughed. "When she was seventeen, she and her boyfriend at the time stole a bottle from my liquor cabinet and proceeded to get shit-faced. She puked her guts out and had the worst hangover. I made her suffer all day by playing loud music and forcing her to do chores around the house.

I thought maybe it would teach her a lesson, but not my Liberty. That child had a rebellious streak a mile long."

"And she still likes bourbon." Miles raised his drink. "But in the short time I've known her, I can't say I've ever seen her hammered."

"Whenever she had to take care of her brother, she was a good kid. I know this is going to sound strange coming from me as I figure you know the whole sordid tale." Harvey took a slow draw from his drink. "But I tried not to make her Gabriel's caretaker when she was a kid. My ex-wife didn't want Gabriel leaving the house, so I hired professionals to come in to help. People who worked with kids on the spectrum. We weren't equipped to deal with it and Liberty was just a child herself. But Robin would always fire the help and make Liberty handle Gabriel. Fucking broke my heart."

"None of this is any of my business and I honestly don't want to talk about this behind her back. I'm seriously trying not to judge you, but you were the parent. You chose those things. They did not."

"Trust me, you're not telling me anything I don't know or haven't lived with all these years." Harvey rested his hands on the counter and held Miles' stare. "This might piss you off, but I wanted to know what I was walking into, so I had my assistant check you out."

"That does annoy me," Miles said.

"Well, all Sandra found was a good man with a solid family." He placed his hand over his backpack. "And truthfully, the only reason I did it was because I didn't want to make the same mistake twice. I knew Charlie was an asshole. There are reasons why I own more of that company and he'll never get it. His father was pissed when I made that deal with Charlie's grandfather, but it was the only way to save Livingston Development." Harvey pulled out a stack of documents. "You can read the deal for yourself." He pushed them across the counter.

Miles took a healthy swig of his bourbon, letting the wood flavor settle on his tongue before swallowing. He glanced at the papers. The sentences jumbled together like a broken jigsaw puzzle with more than half the pieces missing. He could make out a few words here and there. He tapped his finger on the page, trying to make sense of it, but the longer he stared at it, the more his anxiety kicked in, making it worse.

He sighed. "I'm sorry, sir. But either you're going to have to read this to me or explain it."

"Well, son. I can explain it, but I sure as shit can't read it." Harvey chuckled. "I'm fucking dyslexic. Can't read a word on that page. It's a damn miracle I even graduated high school. My father used to call me the dumber of dumb and dumber. And my mom was even worse." He shook his head. "I'll never forget the day I made my first million and bought them a house. The look on my dad's face was classic. His dumbass kid who couldn't read had made it."

"How do they treat you now?" Miles' heart beat in the center of his throat. He'd met other people like him and most struggled like he did. But he'd never met anyone who'd become a billionaire.

"My dad passed away a few years ago and my mom, well, she likes my money and I take care of her, but it's a strained relationship in part because of my ex-wife and in part because of what I did when I abandoned my kids." Harvey's shoulders slumped and he kicked back half of his drink. "I can't believe I'm sitting here about to see Liberty after all these years. I've thought so long and hard about what I would say to her and now that it's about to happen, I've got nothing."

"If it makes you feel any better, I believe Liberty is feeling about the same way."

"I'm sure she'll come in with some pretty colorful language and a lot of anger. All of which I deserve." Harvey ran his hand over his mouth. "I can live with her never forgiving me because I don't expect it and that's not why I'm here. But what I can't live with is sitting around doing nothing anymore. I should have warned her about Charlie, but I didn't know she wasn't getting the money or hadn't read my notes. If I had known that… I would have done so many things differently." He lifted his tumbler. "I know money doesn't make up for shit. But at the time it was all I thought I had."

The sound of the front door opening caught Miles' attention.

Harvey glanced over his shoulder. "I'm not sure I'm ready for this." He downed the last drop of his drink.

Ready or not, it was time to clear up the past, nail Charlie to the wall, and give Liberty, Gabriel, and even Harvey some peace.

$\mathcal{L}$iberty twisted the doorknob to Miles' home and pushed it open. She thought about knocking but decided to just walk in. Maybe she shouldn't. This wasn't her house and while Miles was someone she cared about more than anyone other than her brother, they hadn't defined anything.

She stepped into the family room and paused, staring at her father. He'd aged. His hair was a little thinner and had grayed some. As she inched closer, she noticed the deep-set lines around his bright-blue eyes, which had dulled over the years.

The man she remembered had always looked somewhat tired, but the man sitting in Miles' kitchen, holding an empty glass, looked exhausted. Spent. As if life had beaten him down.

She shouldn't feel sorry for him for a single second.

"Liberty," her father whispered. "You're still the prettiest girl in any room."

As a small child, he would always praise not only her looks, but she did remember him telling her that she could be anything she wanted, if she put her mind to it. However, as she got older, and things with Gabriel became more of a struggle, those compliments were few and far between.

Or were they?

Flashes of her teenage years bombarded her brain.

It had always been her dad who had been there. He'd shown up when she needed him most. Never her mother. She'd always been absent, even when she'd been a small child.

But not her dad.

Until the day he left.

She couldn't erase that if she tried.

Her father stood and gripped her forearm. "Considering all that I've learned, you look good."

"You look like shit," she mumbled, pointing to the bourbon and glancing toward Miles.

"Always the honest one." Her dad let out a short laugh and climbed back on the stool. "I was just expelling to Miles here that while I'm happy to explain the documents I brought, I couldn't read them to him, though not exactly sure why he'd want them read out loud." He reached for the bottle of scotch and poured himself a couple of fingers. He lifted the glass and stared into it as if it had all the answers to the world's problems. "You know, when Liberty was a little girl, she used to come into my home office and I'd be listening to a program that read me contracts. She'd hit the keys on the computer to stop the mechanical voice and say, *Daddy, I'll read them to you.* And we'd sit there and she'd read me my work, and then we'd talk about what I should do. She was always so smart. I used to ask her if she wanted to come work for me someday and you know what she used to say to her old man?"

"Over my dead body." Liberty took the glass Miles handed her and arched a brow. "Dad, for a smart man, sometimes you're not too bright if you can't figure out why Miles would need you to read them."

Miles cocked his head.

Her father sat up taller. "Oh. I guess we have something more in common than wanting to put Charlie behind bars." He raised his drink. "Here's to being the dumber part of dumb."

Miles laughed. "I'll drink to that."

"Oh my God. Neither one of you is stupid. Misguided and you've both done some idiotic things. But dumb you are not." She took a tiny sip. While she needed a shot of courage, she needed to keep her wits about her for this conversation. "Now that we got that cleared up, I need you to answer a few questions."

"That's why I'm here, but first, how's Gabriel? I

need to know," her father said. "I might have been a shit for leaving you, but I'm still his father, and whether you want to believe it or not, I do love him."

"He was shaken up pretty bad and I'm worried he'll have those nightmares he used to get when Mom would lock him in his room." She leaned against the sink, opposite her father. She wanted some distance, but she also wanted to make sure she could read his facial expressions. While her dad was a master of making certain business deals, he wasn't always the best liar.

Unlike her mother.

Then again, he'd known he wasn't her biological dad for years, so what did she know.

"Maybe we should have this conversation at your place so if he wakes up—"

"No." She interrupted her dad. "He's not ready to see you and I don't want him to. I left him a note with instructions to call me. He's not a child anymore. And if he's really that scared, he'll come to Miles anyway."

"All right." Her dad nodded. "What I brought should be enough to put Charlie behind bars. I just wish I had put it all together sooner."

"What is it?" She set her glass down and inched closer to Miles, leaning against his arm. She needed to feel his skin against hers. To absorb his strength.

"His grandfather wanted to cut him out altogether. He and his father were running the company to the ground. They were spending money like it was growing on trees. They bought properties without any real plan. The investments they were making didn't make sense. The old man came to me and asked me to help. Before he left the business, we cut a deal. I bought out most of Livingston Development."

"I have only learned that happened right around the time you left. Why?" Liberty asked.

"My first plan was taking you kids with me to South Carolina where I was opening new offices. Your mother got wind of that and destroyed those plans about the same time Charlie's grandfather came to me. One doesn't have to do with the other." Her father held up his hand. "But my control of the company has everything to do with you, Gabriel, and Charlie."

"I don't understand. Why?" Liberty asked.

Her father tapped the papers. "The deal was that Charlie's grandfather help you get and stay on your feet. Not Charlie or his idiot father. And Old Man Livingston held up his end of the bargain as best he could from what I understand."

"He did. Sort of. I mean, he got me a job and he was nice to me, but if he knew about the money, he said nothing," she said.

"That was between you and me and while he knew I was doing it, I assume he thought better of interfering. When we spoke, which wasn't often, especially after his stroke and he was out of the business, I was left dealing with Charlie and Oswald. I don't like them and was constantly having to deal with their poor decisions to the point that I took voting rights from them."

"I don't mean to butt my nose in where it doesn't belong, but how exactly does this affect Liberty and Gabriel?" Miles asked.

"Because when I retire, or die, my seventy percent and all my voting rights go to them," her father said.

Miles wrapped his arm around her and pulled her close. "You're not married to him anymore so that's null and void."

"I'm shocked he let you go so easily." Her father arched a brow.

"He didn't." She took her glass and tossed it back in one gulp. "Dad, what about this gifting inheritance. Charlie has to be married and have a kid to get his money."

"Sweetheart, there is no money left. The Livingstons are essentially broke. They need you to gain control of my company and that's all they've ever cared about, only I didn't see it until it was too late." Once again, he tapped the papers. "But there's more. If they did anything criminal, anything at all, that thirty percent is mine. It's in the bylaws of the company. It works both ways as in if I did anything illegal, which I haven't. Only I did something just as bad by abandoning you and Gabriel."

"Yeah, that was pretty shitty," she mumbled. "I

can't prove Charlie shoved me down the stairs which caused the death of my child."

"We can prove he locked Gabriel in his house against his will," Miles said. "That's kidnapping and criminal."

"I've got the smoking gun." Her father took out another stack of papers. "I had Sandra, my assistant—"

"Sandra's working for you again?" Liberty asked. Sandra had been in and out of their house since Liberty could remember. Sandra was a kind woman. Sweet. Gentle. Always good with Gabriel and Liberty's mother hated Sandra for that. Never understood why Sandra would even bother.

But her father never once got upset when Sandra would stop to play a game or spend time with his son when she was supposed to be working on some deal.

"She's the only person I trust and she and I have way more in common than we knew," her dad said. "Anyway, when Charlie asked to open the office in Lighthouse Cove and I knew that you had moved here—"

"I'm sorry, how did you know?" Miles asked.

Her father let out a short breath. "I've always known where and what my children were doing. I might not have had the correct information because I was too foolish and hurt to examine everything closely, but I kept tabs on them."

"So, you knew I was pregnant and that I lost my

baby?" Tears stung her eyes, but she wasn't going to cry. Not now. Not in front of her father.

Miles held her closer.

Her dad nodded.

"The anonymous flowers? The basket of my favorite cookies?"

"Yes. That was me," her dad said softly.

"I want to call you a coward." Her heart dropped to the pit of her stomach. She should have known it wasn't an old friend, or even maybe Charlie.

"I'm sure you want to call me all sorts of names." Her father held her stare. "But let's get to how to nail Charlie, and then you can let loose on me, okay?"

She nodded.

"Lighthouse Cove is a unique place. One that shouldn't be overdeveloped, but there are a lot of older homes and lots that could use a light touch. Not to mention the old mall outside of town and the race-track. All untapped real estate that, done right, would bring money without the headaches to this town. I've done similar things to small towns in South Carolina. It's different than what I've done in other places and I certainly wasn't opposed to an office here, but not like Charlie wanted to do. So, when he approached me with the idea, it was under specific guidelines. He's already broken them."

"I'm sorry, sir. That's not criminal," Miles said.

"First, cut the sir crap. My name is Harvey. You

might be sleeping with my daughter, and I am a wealthy man, but that doesn't mean my shit doesn't stink like everyone else," her dad said. "And you're right. It's not. But embezzling money is." He lifted documents from the counter and strolled around the island, shoving them at his daughter. "Take a look. I sent this all to the emails that Miles gave me right when I landed. To be honest, because that last email stated that you and Charlie were working things out, I wasn't going to do anything with this because it would have destroyed someone you cared about and I didn't want to hurt you."

"We have it now and that means it went to my father," Miles said. "He used to be the district attorney, so he'll know what to do with them and that means we got Charlie no matter what."

"Only, he should be going away for murder for what he did to my grandchild." Her father slammed his fist on the counter. "I also blame myself."

"I blame you for a lot of things, Dad. But you didn't push me into Charlie's arms."

"Maybe not," her dad said. "But once he found out that you and Gabriel got everything, he went after you and I left you vulnerable. Even after I knew you married him, I did nothing, except try to catch them at something illegal and even then, I sat on it."

"Because of Charlie's manipulation," Miles said. "He played everyone."

"If it wasn't for Sandra, not only would I not have found half this shit, but I would have never gotten through these last few years."

"Weird random question, Dad. But how did Sandra end up back at Livingston Development? I remember her storming out of the house, screaming at someone and saying she hoped she'd never see you again. Which also begs the question, why did you change the name if you owned controlling interest?"

"Now that's the real shitkicker and some of it I'm not sure you're ready for." He leaned across the counter and grabbed his drink but didn't bring it to his lips. "But secrets are what got us into this mess. It's what caused you to lose your baby and why Gabriel got kidnapped. No more lies." He set the tumbler down and looked directly into her eyes with a tear rolling down his cheek. "I changed the name because I wanted your mother to believe I'd sold out. I wanted her to believe it was us who was in financial ruin. Sandra storming out was part of that game. She helped me hid true ownership of the company, and money from your mother, but because she was going through a divorce herself, she needed to leave my employment."

"Is that why you and mom divorced?" Liberty asked.

"One of many reasons, but mostly I couldn't stand to look at her anymore. However, in the end, she left me before I had the chance to throw her out.

Good thing too, because she was sleeping with some guy she met on a ski trip, which kicked in the prenup and she left with nothing." He sighed.

"And Sandra? Why couldn't she work with you through her divorce?" Liberty asked. She had no idea why she was so fixated on her, but the hammering in her chest told her it was important.

"You might want to sit down for this one," her dad said. "But understand her divorce isn't about you."

"No, I'll stand." She took Miles' hand and gripped it, hard.

"Do you remember Sandra's husband, Kirk?" her dad asked.

Liberty nodded.

"Your mom had an affair with him, as she did many other men. I'm sorry. I don't say this to hurt you and I'm honestly no longer angry about it. But that affair nearly destroyed my working relationship with Sandra, whom I'm lost without. But it's more than that because it was an affair that had happened a long time ago. It had been over for years when we learned of it and when your mom told Sandra, I knew she'd tell you if I tried to take you and Gabriel with me to South Carolina."

"No way." Liberty covered her mouth as her entire body went numb. There was no rage in her veins. Only sadness. "Where's my mother now?"

"She lives in Denver," her father said softly. "If

you ask her, she'd deny it, if she even takes your call. She recently got remarried." Her father closed his eyes. "I'm sorry, Liberty. She told her new husband she didn't have kids."

"Fucking bitch," Liberty muttered. "I hope she rots in hell."

"I've thought worse." Her dad blinked, leaning against the island.

"What about Kirk?" Miles asked. "Does he know?"

Her dad nodded. "We've talked. They were having problems long before all this came out. I reached out to her about five years ago, begging her to come back. She did. She told me that Kirk never once thought Liberty could be his and that once he learned the truth, he couldn't destroy a family, even after I left. He wasn't the man who raised Liberty. That was me and he would never get in the way of that. If Liberty ever wanted to know him, he wouldn't be opposed, but he wouldn't be the one to step in and break that news."

"Well, everything I thought I knew about my life just went fucking sideways." She jerked her hand away and paced in the kitchen. "I'm sorry, Dad. No, wait. I'm not. You people fucked with my life. You lied to me. You abandoned me and Gabriel. And then when you knew Charlie was a shit, you did nothing but a little digging. No amount of anonymous cookies or monthly checks or leaving me a fucking company could ever make up for that."

"I know." Her father took the documents and stacked them into a neat pile on the counter and then flung his backpack over his shoulder. "I didn't come here expecting forgiveness. I'm sure I don't deserve it. I'm just glad I was able to help." Tentatively, he placed his hand on her shoulder. "Please know that the note I left was my stupid way of telling you that I'd always be there for you, no matter what. That you could always reach out. It's why, even though I know now it wasn't you emailing me, that I always responded. Money doesn't solve most problems, but please let me continue to give you and Gabriel some of mine. Lord knows I have more than I know what to do with." He jerked his thumb toward Miles. "That one over there seems like a good man who cares a great deal for you and Gabriel. As you comb through those documents with him, you should remind him of what you used to tell me when I used to get frustrated."

A slow smile spread across her face at the memory. "That understanding the information is always more important than being able to read it because words on the page are meaningless unless you know what to do with them after they've been said."

"Best advice I've ever been given." He leaned in and kissed her forehead, like he used to do when she'd been little. "Miles was kind enough to find me a room at a local B and B. I'll be staying there until Charlie is arrested, and then I'll fly back to South Carolina. The only place I'll be is there and the Livingston Development offices, so you won't have to worry about me running into Gabriel. I know that won't be good for him." He turned and stretched out his arm. "Take care of my little girl and keep me informed of what happens with Charlie."

Miles took her father's hand. "I'll do that."

"Thank you."

Her dad turned and headed toward the door.

"Dad. Wait." She sucked in a deep breath. "Thank you."

"You're welcome," he said. "If you ever need me or just want to talk, I won't ever say no." With that, her father walked out the door.

Miles came up behind her and put his arms around her middle. "You doing okay?"

"No. Yes. Fuck if I know."

Miles twisted her body until she was facing him dead-on. "I'm not defending what your father did, because some of it is just plain wrong. But he was living his own hell. He was trapped in a loveless marriage—"

She covered Miles' mouth. "I know. I lived it. And a million and one memories, both good and bad, have filled my brain. But I can't reconcile the fact he still left."

"Look. Your father is a broken man. He has to live with what he's done for the rest of his life."

"You can't seriously be asking me to forgive him just because he came forward with this information?" She cocked her head.

"No. But I am asking you to show him a little compassion," Miles said. "Just like I asked Jameson to show our mother when she told us about her affair and who Jameson's biological father was. What our parents did was wrong. Dead wrong. And it fucked with all of us. We can't go back and change history. But we can learn from it. We can accept it and move forward. Your dad has never forgotten. In his own weird, messed-up way, he's been there for you and Gabriel. Charlie—and frankly, your mother—got in the way of that and if they hadn't, who knows. Maybe the three of you might have stood a chance at reconciling a long time ago."

She cupped Miles' cheek. "Information is always more important—"

He pressed his fingers on her lips. "I really want to believe I'm good enough for you. For Gabriel. Those old tapes are hard to stop." He kissed her softly. "I'm falling so hard for you, Liberty; it's making my head spin."

"You and me both," she whispered, resting her head on his shoulder. "I'm the one who should be worried about being good enough. All I've ever done is take from you."

"Not true." He held her so close, she could feel his heart beating next to hers. "You've given me something no one else ever has."

"What's that?"

"Something to love." He tilted her chin with his thumb and forefinger. "I've never been in love before, but I think I'm in love with you."

"Well, stop thinking and start feeling, because I know I'm in love with you." Before she could press her lips against his, Emmerson came barreling through the front door.

"Sorry to interrupt," Emmerson said. "But I have breaking news almost as important as my little brother losing his heart to the best damn thing that has ever happened to him."

"Fuck off," Miles muttered.

"Not on your life and it's about damn time." Emmerson laughed. "But I thought the two of you should know that the State Police, with the help of Mom and Nathan, just arrested Charlie. The charges are extensive and they bleed over to his father, who was picked up five minutes ago. Since it's Friday, those two will be spending the weekend in a jail cell."

"But they will get out on bail, right?" Liberty asked.

"It's possible," Emmerson said, waving his finger. "But our dad spoke to the DA and since they both booked a flight out of the country twenty minutes before they were picked up, they are considered a flight risk. Their bond will be quite high and I heard they were broke, so not likely." Emmerson shook his head. "I only got a peek at what was in those documents, but whoever this Sandra person is, Rhett wants to hire her. She found hidden bank accounts that prove Charlie and his father were stealing money from Liberty's dad for years. She only started flagging it when she went back to work for him a few years ago. Your dad's been working on this for quite some time."

"I wonder why he didn't tell us all that," Miles said.

"Because my dad's a proud man." She patted Miles' chest. "Sandra understood his learning disability and helped him hide it from everyone else. My mom always made him feel like he was stupid, like my grandparents did, and he didn't want anyone in the company to know. So the fact that Charlie and Oswald were able to exploit that, I'm sure burns my father's ass and makes him feel foolish because he couldn't see it in black and white. He's like you that way. He relied on me and Sandra to help him. He lost me when he left us, and Sandra too, leaving him with my mother, who was trying to take him for every penny he earned the old-fashioned way."

"He had to have someone helping him," Miles said.

"My father was always resourceful and it sounds like Sandra was always helping. But, like you, he senses when things are amiss and that's when he begged Sandra to come back full-time." She raced to the island and shuffled through some of the paperwork, sorting through it by date until she found what she was looking for. "It all comes back to when I lost my baby." She shoved the paperwork at Miles, who handed it to his brother. "The divorce attorney that landed in my lap. That wasn't by accident. Sandra set that up, which means my father had a hand in that. Jesus, why wouldn't he just come out and say that?"

"Pride. Shame," Emmerson said. "And I could think of a million other reasons why he wouldn't, including not wanting it to be seen as meddling, but let's be glad that he did."

"Not to mention he knows that you'd see all that anyway," Miles said. "He doesn't believe what he did is forgivable. All he wants is to do what he can to make up for it. And in a way, he did."

"None of this is making it easy for me to continuing hating that man." She tossed the papers back on the island. "Because I want to."

"Forgiveness comes in stages. Ask our brother Jameson about that." Emmerson squeezed her shoulder. "I need to go back to my wife. They are releasing her tomorrow and while she's as cool as a cucumber about having twins and this whole needing extra fluids thing until the morning sickness goes away, I'm a fucking wreck."

Liberty laughed. "Emmerson, you're going to be a

great dad and Miles is going to be the best godfather known to man."

"If he doesn't drop one of my kids on his head." Emmerson slapped his brother on the back. "You two can sleep easy tonight." He waggled his finger. "Don't do anything I wouldn't do."

"Well, that doesn't leave us much. I was hoping to use some handcuffs," Miles said.

"Go right ahead, little brother." Emmerson laughed. "See ya later, lovebirds." Emmerson turned on a dime and strolled out the door.

"Handcuffs?" Liberty asked.

"Inside joke, but damn, he finally did it again."

"I don't think I want to know."

Miles took her by the hand. "Come on. You should be at home in case Gabriel wakes up. I can sleep on the sofa if you want me to. But even though Charlie has been arrested, I'm not leaving your house."

"I think it's safe to say that my bed would be an acceptable place for you to crash for the night," she said. "But what am I supposed to do about my dad?"

"Nothing tonight." He kissed her palm. "My brother's right. Whatever happens with your dad will come in stages. There is a world of hurt and it's not going away overnight."

She paused at the front door and gazed into the one man's eyes whom she knew without a shadow of a doubt would never intentionally hurt her or her brother. Miles was hers to love. "I'm never getting a real date out of you because we're way beyond that now."

"Oh, no, we are not. I'm still doing that right no matter how we feel about each other. You deserve the world and I plan on giving it to you."

## 15

*L*iberty sipped her coffee and stared at the two men she loved the most.

Miles and her brother.

Gabriel scarfed down his bowl of cereal like he hadn't eaten in days, while Miles pressed an earbud in his ear and listened to the news.

They hadn't kept anything about Charlie or Oswald's arrests from Gabriel, but she had wanted to keep her father's return from her brother.

Yet in the morning light, she wasn't so sure.

She'd tossed and turned all night, thinking about all the things her father had done, both good and bad. She'd slipped from the bed at three in the morning and googled her mother. What she'd found had been utterly horrifying. That bitch had changed her name and her history, erasing her dad, her, and Gabriel from her life. She'd created a completely new identity for herself and now lived in Denver, married to some man twelve years younger than her, helping to raise his three kids.

Bitch wasn't a strong enough word.

When Miles had found her, he tried to stop her from continuing down the rabbit hole, but she was obsessed. So, he sent a message to his brother, Rhett. Who found out even more.

It had been her mother who had gone to Charlie. Her mom who had informed Charlie of the deal her father made with Old Man Livingston. And her mother had her own deal with Charlie. She got a payout when Charlie got his hands on Livingston Development.

The problem, though, was she'd done nothing illegal and there wasn't a damn thing she could do to her mother. Miles had told her through the wee hours of the morning that karma was a bitch and karma would catch her mom eventually.

God, she hoped so.

She leaned across the counter and pulled out Miles' earbud.

"Hey. I was listening to that." He glared.

"I might need a little help with something." She turned her attention to her brother. "Gabriel, I need to talk to you about something."

"I really hate it when you start conversations like that." Gabriel dropped his spoon in his bowl. "And if you're going to treat me like a child, I'm going to go play video games."

"I'm not going to do that," she said. "Now that Charlie has been arrested and is out of our lives, I need to tell you how that was possible, because I don't want secrets between us."

Miles set his phone on the counter and cocked a brow. "Are you sure you want to do this?"

"As sure as I'm in love with you." She sipped her coffee, daring him to comment on that.

He didn't.

But Gabriel smiled like a big kid in a candy store. "Love. That's a big word."

"It is and I wouldn't use it if I didn't mean it," she said.

"Do you love my sister?" Gabriel asked, staring at Miles.

"I do." Miles nodded. "And I love you too."

"We're a package deal," Gabriel said. "But if you hurt my sister, I'm coming for you."

Miles wiped his face with his hand. "I hope that never happens."

"Okay. Now that we have that out of the way," Liberty said. "While Miles' family was looking for you, we had to do some digging to find out all the things that Charlie was doing that were illegal, which led us way back into the past."

"Don't talk in circles. I hate that." Gabriel fisted his hands.

"All right. I had to reach out to Dad," she said matter-of-factly.

"Daddy? You spoke to our dad?" Gabriel asked softly as he rocked back and forth. "Did you talk to Mom too?"

"I did not."

"Good." Gabriel let out a long breath. "I don't like Mom. She was mean. She locked me in my bedroom when people came over and wouldn't let me out. But Daddy would come in and play games with me. He would tell me that he thought Mommy was mean too and that he didn't want to hang out with those stuffy people anyway."

Liberty gasped. "You never told me that before."

"You never asked." Gabriel stopped rocking.

"I guess I didn't," she said. "You should know that Mom and Dad are divorced and they don't speak at all anymore."

"Good for Dad." Gabriel nodded.

This was not what she expected from her little brother.

"Mommy was so mean to Dad. She called him stupid. I don't know why. He was always so smart." Gabriel smiled. "But he could never beat me at chess. I was too good, even for him."

Miles chuckled. "You are a wizard when it comes to that game, that's for sure."

"Anyway. I saw Dad. I got to speak with him and while I can't forgive him for leaving us, I don't have the right to make that decision for you." She reached out and took her brother's hand. "He's in Lighthouse Cove and I know he'd like to see you. That is if you want to see him."

"You'd let me?" Gabriel blinked.

"It's not for me to decide," she said.

"What do you think I should do? I mean, he left us alone. He left you to take care of me. I know you've always said you never minded, but I also know you don't like him much for doing that." Gabriel rubbed his hands on his shirt.

"Our father has made a lot of mistakes. Some of them were to protect us from our mother. And others were because after he left, he felt like he couldn't come back." She squeezed her brother's hand. "I'm not going to stand in the way of you getting to know Dad again, if that's what you want."

"Miles?" Gabriel turned his head. "What's your feeling on this?"

"Buddy, my opinion doesn't matter," Miles said.

"It does to him." Liberty glared.

"Okay." Miles let out a long breath. "If you want to see your dad, then you should. My only advice would be to leave the past where it belongs and start fresh." He lifted his gaze. "That goes for both of you."

"I want to see my dad." Gabriel stood. "I'll go get dressed." Gabriel raced toward the stairs.

"I guess I better call my father and tell him we're

coming." Liberty picked up her cell and tapped her dad's number.

Straight to voicemail.

"Maybe he's in the shower," Miles said. "Call the B and B. Melinda will patch you through to his room."

Liberty found the number and Melinda answered on the second ring.

"Hi. This is Liberty Blue. I'm trying to reach my father. Harvey Blue." Liberty's heart hammered in her chest.

"I'm sorry, but he checked out a half hour ago. I think he was headed to the airport."

Miles was on his feet. "He came by private jet. I'll get my mom to stop him. Let's go."

"She can do that?"

"She's the chief of police. At least for two more weeks. She can do anything she wants, within reason." Miles moved to the bottom of the stairs. "Hurry up, Gabriel. We have to roll, now."

"You really are my knight in shining armor."

Miles laughed. "I'm just a grease monkey who has family in high places."

Liberty's heart beat so fast it caught in her throat as they pulled into the private airport twenty-five miles from Lighthouse Cove. Her father's plane, which still had the words, *Liberty Gabriel* proudly displayed on the side, was parked not far from the runway.

"Well, that's a bold statement." Miles took her hand and kissed it. "He never forgot."

"I still want to hate him," she mumbled. "Those are just letters on metal."

"That mean something when said out loud." He kissed her hand before glancing over his shoulder. "Are you ready?"

"What do I say?" Gabriel asked.

"Whatever you feel like," Miles said. He opened the door.

Liberty slid from the passenger seat and few seconds later, her father appeared at the entrance of the plane. He climbed down the stairs and took two steps across the pavement.

Gabriel bolted from the back of Miles' truck. "Daddy!" He ran like a big goofy kid with his arms flapping wildly at his sides. "Daddy!"

Her six-foot-three dad stopped dead in his tracks as Gabriel, all five foot ten and one hundred ninety pounds of him came barreling at him. Her dad reached for the railing of the airplane's staircase but missed and lost his footing.

"You came back." Gabriel hurled himself at his father, wrapping his arms around him, knocking them both to the hard ground with a massive thud.

"Shit." Liberty took off running, Miles at her heels.

"Gabriel. Dad. Are you two okay?" She knelt, trying to untangle her brother from her dad, but Gabriel wouldn't let him go.

Her father grunted as he lay flat on his back. "Gabriel, son, you're crushing me."

"Let me help." Miles did his best to unwrap Gabriel's arms, but even he couldn't do it. "Gabriel, dude. You've got to give your dad some breathing room."

Reluctantly, Gabriel eased his grip and rolled to the side.

"Damn, boy. You've grown." Her dad took Miles' hand and slowly got to his feet, arching his back.

"Anything broken?" Miles asked.

"Nah. I'll live," her dad said, hoisting Gabriel off the pavement. "Let me get a good look at you." He held Gabriel by the shoulders. "Wow. You're all grown up." He ruffled Gabriel's hair.

"Dad. Stop that. I'm not a little boy anymore. I'm a man." Gabriel pushed his father's hand away.

Her dad chuckled. "I can see that."

"I should be so mad at you." He stomped his feet and clenched his fists. "What you did was wrong. You hurt Liberty. She ended up marrying a very bad man because of you and Charlie hurt her in the worst way. I should hate you for that. But I don't." He slumped his shoulders and relaxed his hands. "I've missed you."

"I've missed you and your sister so much." Her

dad rested his hand on Gabriel's shoulder. He'd always had a way with him, even she couldn't deny that. "I'm sorry I left you. I wish I could go back in time and do it all over again, but I'm so glad you two had each other."

"Why are you leaving again?" Gabriel sniffled.

Her dad shifted his gaze from him to her and cleared his throat. "I don't have to, but to be honest, Gabriel, that's going to be up to Liberty."

"Oh, no, you don't. You can't put this one on me," she mumbled.

"I have to." He palmed her face. "You've been the one taking care of both of you all these years. It's not my place anymore to waltz into your life like I belong." He kissed her temple. "I will stay, but only if you say it's okay," he whispered.

She closed her eyes and wrapped her arms around her dad.

Her father.

"It's okay," she said.

Her dad hugged her back.

She took a step back. "How long can you stay?"

"As long as you'll have me. Someone has to run the office here now." He shrugged. "But I'd have to go back and forth between here and South Carolina for a while and there is Sandra to consider."

"I'm sure she can help you remotely," Liberty said.

Her father shook his head. "We're engaged, so she would be coming with me."

"Well, that's an interesting turn of events." Liberty smiled.

"I like Sandra." Gabriel looped his arm through Liberty's. "So, Miles, when are you going to ask my sister to marry you?"

"Yeah, son. When's that happening?" Her dad smacked Miles on the back.

He coughed, pounding on his chest.

All she could do was grin from ear to ear.

Not all was forgiven.

But the past was behind them.

This was a fresh start. A clean slate. A new beginning.

And Miles was hers to love.

FOUR MONTHS LATER...

"Let me get that." Miles took the tray from Rumor. "Where is your idiot husband anyway?"

"You mean your brother?" Rumor laughed. "Chained to the bed."

Miles nearly dropped the tray of drinks.

"I'm joking." She patted Miles' back. "He's arguing with your mother about baby names."

"Good luck with that." Miles set the tray on the table and kissed Liberty's sweet lips. "Here you go."

"Why, thank you." She took the cocktail and sipped. "Damn, Emmerson makes a mean margarita."

"He sure does." Miles straddled one of the chairs and waved to Gabriel. "He looks perplexed."

"He's about to lose his first game of chess to my

dad." Liberty laughed. "Never thought I'd enjoy having that man back in my life, but dammit, I do."

"He's not the worst person in the world," Miles said.

"Nope. He's not." Liberty sipped her drink. "And now that Charlie and his father have been sentenced to thirty years in prison, we all can really rest easy."

"We sure can." Miles had never been more grateful than when that sentence had been handed down. "Steven's niece, Stephanie, is totally enamored by Gabriel. It's kind of cute."

"He likes her too and I hate to admit it, but she's good for him," Liberty said. "Helps him even out his emotions. I just hope things keep going slowly."

"What's slow? Because I saw them kissing in the garage," Rumor said. "Might have been some fondling."

"Wonderful. I'm so not ready for that," Liberty sighed. "So, Rumor, how are you feeling these days?"

"Well, the morning sickness is completely gone, but these two rascals are already kicking the hell out of my bladder." She patted her rounded belly. "I get up like five times a night to pee and it makes Emmerson crazy. The man is the biggest worrywart."

"I can't say as I blame him," Miles said. "He nearly lost you when you got shot and then the scare with the twins. He's been walking on eggshells ever since."

"Doc says these babies are healthy." Rumor

stretched out her legs on the lounge chair. "I hope Emmerson isn't getting too bad of an earful about our name choices. She can be one tough nut."

"You picked names?" Liberty smiled. "Are you going to tell us?"

Rumor nodded. "Our little girl will be Bethany Blue."

Liberty swallowed. Hard. "You're going to use my last name as your child's middle name? I don't know what to even think about that."

"We love the ring to it. And you're special to us." Rumor glanced over her shoulder. "And our little boy will be Benjamin Gabriel."

Liberty fanned her face. "You sure do know how to make a girl cry."

"Aw. Didn't mean to do that," Rumor said. "Miles, have you shown her—"

"Not yet." Miles hopped to his feet. "Come on. Let's go for a walk."

"Where?" Liberty took his hand.

He didn't say a single word. Not because he didn't want to, but because he didn't even know where to begin. They had settled into a nice life together. Well, as best they could living next door to one another while she mended fences with her father and continued to help Gabriel adjust to all the changes.

Gabriel always came first and Miles accepted that.

He never felt as though he were second fiddle to anything.

But sometimes it was hard when he slept alone, in his bed, in his house, instead of with her in his arms. It didn't happen all the time, but it happened enough and he had grown tired of it.

Time for another change.

He placed his hand on the small of her back and guided her around the side of Emmerson's house to the next-door neighbor's, which was currently empty and for sale. He tapped his fingers on the keypad, punching in the code that the real estate agent had given him.

"Miles, what the hell are you doing?" Liberty tugged at his arm.

"I wanted to show you this place."

"Why?"

He pushed open the door and gave her a little shove. His brother Jameson had just finished the renovation on it for the owners and he'd done a bang-up job. The layout was similar to Emmerson's, although it didn't have a pool house. But it did have a tiki bar, which was cool.

And his neighbor would be his brother.

That was if Liberty went for it.

All of it.

"Because I want to buy it." He took her hand and led her into the spacious kitchen where he'd left some paperwork for her to look at. Talk about a little secret.

"Are you kidding me? I bet the listing for this place is over two million."

"It's actually close to three," he said.

"How can you afford this?"

"Not me. Us." He tapped his finger on the papers, which was held down by an engagement ring. He wasn't the most romantic, and neither was Liberty. The whole *on one knee* thing wasn't going to work for her, so he wasn't going to do it. Subtle was more her style.

And his.

She pushed the ring to the side as if she hadn't even seen it.

He chuckled.

Figures.

"What am I looking at?"

"My bank statements." He leaned against the counter, taking the ring into his hands, fiddling with it. "I know someone who is interested in buying my house now that all the renovations are complete and Jameson is dying to get his hands on yours. He figures he can be done with it in four months and we should be able to sell it quickly."

She snapped her gaze to meet his. "Are you suggesting we move in together?"

"Something like that." He held the ring up where he knew she could see it, but she pushed his arm to the counter.

"I can't afford anything like this and I'm not sure how you can either."

"If you would look at the numbers on that paper,

you'd see that clearly, we can afford this place." Once again, he lifted the ring, but this time he'd wait a second before actually shoving it in her face.

Her eyes shifted back and forth as she studied the paper before it slipped from her fingers and a gasp escaped her lips. "Jesus, Miles. That's a whopper of a bottom line."

"I know."

"When you told me you had a little money saved up, that's not what I expected."

He chuckled. "When Trixi's father called me nothing but a grease monkey and a loser and that I'd never be able to take care of a family, I started hoarding money. Part of me did it subconsciously. I'd put it away and forget about it. I don't need much. But now I do have you and Gabriel to think about and maybe sometime we'll have kids of our own."

"Kids of our what now?" She lowered her chin. "How did we go from the fact that you're kind of a millionaire to us having kids? I haven't agreed to move in with you. We're not even married, much less engaged."

He pushed the ring up to her face. "But we could be. That is if you'll have the dumber part of dumb."

"Holy shit." She plucked the ring from his fingers. "Miles Rutherford Kirby, what have you gone and done?"

"I think that's obvious," he whispered. "I love you

and I want to spend the rest of my life showing you that I'm good enough."

"Wow." She slipped the ring on and wiggled her fingers in front of her face.

"Is that a yes?"

"You know I'm not the only person you have to ask." She rested her hands on his shoulders.

"Who the fuck do you think helped me pick out that ring?" He arched a brow.

"No way. Gabriel knew and he kept it a secret? From me? His only sister? For how long?"

"Three long fucking weeks." He brushed his lips over her mouth.

"Oh my God. When we go back to Emmerson's, they're all going to be staring at my finger to see if you put a ring on it, aren't they?"

"Not only that, but the rest of my family will be there with cake. It's a whole thing."

She stepped back and poked him in the chest.

"Ouch. What did you do that for?"

"You're a sneaky devil. And what would have happened if I said no?"

"I was fairly confident you would say yes to marriage, but not so much on the house. I still don't know what you think about this place."

"Again, it's Gabriel—"

He covered her mouth. "Don't get mad. But he's seen it and knows I want to buy it. For us. For our family. Come on, Liberty. What do you say?"

"At least this time the man I picked, his only ulterior motive is to get into my pants."

"Every chance I get."

She wrapped her arms around his body. "I say yes to it all, but if you ever hide money from me again, I'll deck you."

"You do know that from now on, you'll have to manage all that because Trinity isn't going to want to do it anymore now that I'm going to have a wife." He burst out laughing. "Every time she told me what I was worth, I thought she was fucking with me."

"She's not."

"Good to know. Now, would you like to christen this place?" He waggled his brows.

"Um. No. Everyone would know what we were doing if we took that long. Including my father, Gabriel, and I guess what I should accept as his girlfriend. That's the kind of embarrassment I can't handle right now." She took his hand and yanked him toward the door. "But I can promise you that you'll get some serious action tonight."

Miles followed her back to his brother's house and as soon as they walked through the side gate, everyone stopped and stared.

Liberty raised her hand, showing off her ring.

Gabriel was the first on his feet, congratulating them.

If anyone had asked Miles a year ago if he'd ever settle down, it would have been a hard no. But he hadn't met Liberty yet and she had changed the way he viewed the world.

And himself.

Love wasn't always about taking care of someone. It was about trusting a partnership and that's what he had with Liberty.

# EPILOGUE

## ONE YEAR LATER...

"Hey, I'm home." Miles dropped his keys on the small table by the garage door and followed the noise. "Gabriel, where's your sister?"

Gabriel glanced over his shoulder after pausing his video game. Stephanie, his girlfriend for one full year, sat next to him on the sofa. Her family had moved to Lighthouse Cove six months ago, after Harvey had sold them a small place not too far from Steve.

About that time, Gabriel had started spending two days a week at the development company with his father and the rest of the week, he still worked at the shop with Miles.

Gabriel thrived in both environments, as long as he didn't have to deal too much with people.

And he wasn't made to feel like he was choosing between his dad and Miles.

Which neither man would do.

But now there was Kirk, Liberty's biological father. Gabriel understood what that meant and he also comprehended that Liberty didn't see Kirk that way. That Harvey was father to them both, in all areas that mattered. However, she still wanted to know Kirk. To make a connection to the man whose biology had created her and since they had been talking about having a child, that discussion had become a little more intense.

"In your bedroom," Gabriel said. "She was already here when Dad and I got home."

"Oh, hello." Harvey stepped from kitchen. "I hope you don't mind." He lifted a glass of scotch. "Liberty must have caught a bug because she was white as a ghost when I brought Gabriel home. I ordered pizza since she said she wasn't cooking and I kind of asked Sandra to come over too."

"That's fine. You're both always welcome." He rubbed the back of his neck. "She hasn't been feeling well all week. She had a doctor's appointment earlier. I better go check on her." Although that appointment was all about going off birth control and female stuff that Miles didn't even pretend to understand.

"Well, when you're done with that, why don't you join Gabriel, Stephanie, and me in some video games."

"I might do that." Miles strolled toward the master bedroom where he found Liberty in bed.

"Hey, you," he whispered, sitting on the edge of the mattress. "What's going on?"

"More like what's coming up."

"Okay. I'll keep my distance." He stood.

She chuckled.

"Not funny. I can't afford to be sick."

"I'm not sick." She waved her hand over the nightstand. "Grab that."

He lifted a piece of paper. "Oh. I've seen this before. Emmerson showed me one of these when he found out Rumor was having…" Miles went to sit back on the bed but missed and landed on the floor with a *thud*. "Please tell me you're not having twins."

"There is only one baby in my belly." She patted the top of his head. "Daddy."

He pushed to his feet and eased back onto the bed, resting his hand on her stomach. "Seriously? You're pregnant? And why did you have an ultrasound so fast? Are you okay? Is the baby okay? And how did this happen? You haven't even gone off birth control."

"You sound upset."

"No, babe. Not at all. Just confused. Scared. And maybe a little freaked out."

"Well, it turns out our birth control failed like two months ago and the doctor pressed my belly and was like, hmmm, feels like your uterus has expanded. Let's take a look and holy shit, there's a baby in there." She pushed to a sitting position and kissed his lips. "Turns out you have super sperm to go with your other superpowers."

"I guess so." He bent over and lifted the picture, running his finger over the image. "I'm sorry, but our baby looks like a blob."

"Yeah, that's what I said." She bit down on her fingernail.

He cocked his head. "What am I missing?"

"I'm actually feeling okay. I mean, I was a little queasy this morning, but that was a ruse so I could get you alone while the rest of your family sneaks into the house for a little congratulations party."

Miles arched a brow. "Your dad, Gabriel, and even Stephanie already knew? My mother knows?"

"Everyone knows." She covered his mouth. "But only because when I was walking out of the pharmacy with a handful of prenatal vitamins, I ran into your mom, Trinity, Bryn, and Shelby. It's impossible to lie to those people. Next thing I knew, we were having a party."

He cupped her face. "As long as we don't let my mother name our kid, it's all good."

"About that." She pursed her lips. "I have some ideas about names and before your mom, or anyone else for that matter, even starts, I want you to hear my ideas."

"I'm barely wrapping my brain around being a dad, and you want me to commit to names?"

"Just hear me out."

"All right. Lay them on me."

"If it's a boy, I want to name him Harvey Kirkland Kirby." She lifted her finger. "Before you go shooting it down. Gabriel's never going to have children so my father's never going to have his name carried on. This way he can. And while Kirk isn't my dad in any way that matters, biology does mean something. And he's been incredibly understanding about all of this. Also, knowing that his and Sandra's divorce had nothing to do with me was such a relief."

"Are you done?"

She nodded.

Miles couldn't love his wife anymore if he tried. "I love the name. It works for me. Now, what if it's a girl?"

"This one I'm afraid you might not be on board with, but I want you to consider that it's important to me because this person has been so incredible to Gabriel. And she was the one who—"

"You've got to be kidding me." Miles smacked his forehead. "You seriously want to name a girl Rebecca after my mother? Do you have any idea how that's going to play out?"

"I know how your mom can get, but she's been incredible to me." Liberty held his hand over her stomach.

How could he say no to that? "And the middle name?"

"You can choose that."

"If you leave it up to me, her name will be Rebecca Francis Kirby." Miles chuckled.

"Why Francis?"

"That's what I named my first car."

"Oh my God." She cupped his face. "Rebecca Francis it is."

"My mother's going to hate that because she despised that vehicle." Miles pulled back the covers and climbed in next to his wife. "It was a beat-up old Gremlin. Puke green and I was so freaking proud of it. First car I restored to its original glory. Took me five months, but I had her purring like a kitten."

"What happened to her?"

Miles shook his head. "She's still in my shop. No way would I ever part with my first love."

"Well, now you have me." Liberty pressed his hand over her belly. "And our little baby."

"Something for both of us to love."


Thank you for taking the time to read MINE TO LOVE. Feel free to leave an honest review. This is the last book in the Safe Harbor Series. If you're looking for another small town series with strong family ties (thought a bit dysfunctional), lots of drama, and tinge of suspense, check out my Emerald City Series.

*Investigate Away*
*Sail Away*
*Fly Away*
*Flirt Away*

Grab a glass of vino, kick back, relax, and let the romance roll in…

*Sign up for my Newsletter (https://dl.bookfunnel.com/82gm8b9k4y) where I often give away free books before publication.*

*Join my private Facebook group (https://www.facebook.com/groups/191706547909047/) where I post exclusive excerpts and discuss all things murder and love!*

# ABOUT THE AUTHOR

Jen Talty is the *USA Today* Bestselling Author of Contemporary Romance, Romantic Suspense, and Paranormal Romance. In the fall of 2020, her short story was selected and featured in a 1001 Dark Nights Anthology.

Regardless of the genre, her goal is to take you on a ride that will leave you floating under the sun with warmth in your heart. She writes stories about broken heroes and heroines who aren't necessarily looking for romance, but in the end, they find the kind of love books are written about :).

She first started writing while carting her kids to one hockey rink after the other, averaging 170 games per year between 3 kids in 2 countries and 5 states. Her first book, IN TWO WEEKS was originally published in 2007. In 2010 she helped form a publishing company (Cool Gus Publishing) with *NY Times* Bestselling Author Bob Mayer where she ran the technical side of the business through 2016.

Jen is currently enjoying the next phase of her life… the empty nester! She and her husband reside in Jupiter, Florida.

Grab a glass of vino, kick back, relax, and let the romance roll in…

*Sign up for my Newsletter (https://dl.bookfunnel.com/82gm8b9k4y). where I often give away free books before publication.*

*Join my private Facebook group (https://www.facebook.com/groups/191706547909047/) where I post exclusive excerpts and discuss all things murder and love!*

Never miss a new release. Follow me on Amazon:amazon.com/author/jentalty

And on Bookbub: bookbub.com/authors/jen-talty

*To Protect His own*

*Deadly Seduction*

*When A Stranger Calls*

*His Deadly Past*

*The Corkscrew Killer*


*First Responders: A spin-off from the NY State Troopers series*

*Playing With Fire*

*Private Conversation*

*The Right Groom*

*After The Fire*

*Caught In The Flames*

*Chasing The Fire*


*Legacy Series*

*Dark Legacy*

*Legacy of Lies*

*Secret Legacy*


*Emerald City*

*Investigate Away*

*Sail Away*

*Fly Away*

*Flirt Away*

*Colorado Brotherhood Protectors*

*Fighting For Esme*

*Defending Raven*

*Fay's Six*

*Darius' Promise*


*Yellowstone Brotherhood Protectors*

*Guarding Payton*

*Wyatt's Mission*

*Corbin's Mission*


*Candlewood Falls*

*Rivers Edge*

*The Buried Secret*

*Its In His Kiss*

*Lips Of An Angel*

*Kisses Sweeter than Wine*

*A Little Bit Whiskey*


*It's all in the Whiskey*

*Johnnie Walker*

*Georgia Moon*

*Jack Daniels*

*Jim Beam*

*Whiskey Sour*

*Talon's Honor*

*Arthur's Honor*

*Rex's Honor*

*Kent's Honor*

*Aegis Network Short Stories*

*Max & Milian*

*A Christmas Miracle*

*Spinning Wheels*

*Holiday's Vacation*

*The Brotherhood Protectors*

*Out of the Wild*

*Rough Justice*

*Rough Around The Edges*

*Rough Ride*

*Rough Edge*

*Rough Beauty*

*The Brotherhood Protectors*

*The Saving Series*

*Saving Love*

*Saving Magnolia*

*Saving Leather*

*Hot Hunks*

*Cove's Blind Date Blows Up*

*My Everyday Hero – Ledger*

*Tempting Tavor*

*Malachi's Mystic Assignment*

*Needing Neor*

*Holiday Romances*

*A Christmas Getaway*

*Alaskan Christmas*

*Whispers*

*Christmas In The Sand*

*Heroes & Heroines on the Field*

*Taking A Risk*

*Tee Time*

*A New Dawn*

*The Blind Date*

*Spring Fling*

*Summers Gone*

*Winter Wedding*

*The Awakening*

*The Collective Order*

*The Lost Sister*

*The Lost Soldier*

*The Lost Soul*

*The Lost Connection*

*The New Order*